THE BOY SCOUT
AUTOMOBILISTS

BY

ROBERT MAITLAND

The Boy Scout Automobilists

CHAPTER I

CALLED TO ACTIVE SERVICE

"What's this call for a special meeting of the Boy Scouts, Jack?" asked Pete Stubbs, a First Class Boy Scout, of his chum Jack Danby, who had just been appointed Assistant Patrol Leader of the Crow Patrol of the Thirty-ninth Troop.

"Well, I guess it isn't a secret any more," said Jack.

He and Pete Stubbs worked in the same place, and they were great chums, especially since Jack had enlisted his chum in the Boy Scouts.

"The fact is," he continued, "that Scout-Master Durland has been trying for several days to arrange the biggest treat the Troop, or any other Troop, has ever had. You know the State militia begins maneuvers pretty soon, Pete?"

"Say, Jack," cried red-haired Pete, dancing up and down in his excitement, "you don't mean to say that there's a chance that we are to go out with the militia?"

"I think this call means that there's more than a chance, Pete, and that the whole business is settled. You see, some of the fellows work in places where they might find it hard to get off. In the militia it's different. The law makes an employer give a man time off for the militia when it's necessary, but there's no reason why it should be that way for us. But Mr. Durland has been trying to get permission for all of us."

"I'll bet he didn't have any trouble here when he came to see Mr. Simms," said Pete, enthusiastically. "If all the bosses were like him, we'd be all right."

"They're not, Pete, though I guess most of them try to do what's fair, when they understand just how things are. But, anyhow, Mr. Simms thought it was a fine idea, and he went around and helped Mr. Durland with the other people, who weren't so ready to let off the Boy Scouts who happened to be working for them. And I guess that this call means that it's all fixed up, for if it hadn't been nothing would have been said about it."

Pete and Jack, with the other members of the Troop, reported at Scout headquarters that night, and gave Scout-Master Durland a noisy welcome when he rose to address them.

"Now," he said, "I want you to be quiet and listen to me. A great honor has been paid to the Troop. We have been invited to take part, as Scouts, in the coming maneuvers of the National Guard. There is to be a sham war, you know, and the militia of this State and the neighboring State, with some help from the regular army, are to take part in it. A troop of Boy Scouts has been selected from the other State, and after the militia officers had inspected all the Troops in this State they chose the Thirty-ninth."

He had to stop then for a minute to give the great cheer that greeted his announcement time to die away.

"Gee, Jack, I guess we're all right, what?" asked Pete, happily.

"Be still a minute, Pete. Mr. Durland isn't through yet."

"Now, I have gone around and got permission for all of you to go on this trip," the Scout-Master went on. "It's going to be different from anything we've ever done before. It's a great big experiment, and we're going to be watched by Boy Scouts and army and National Guard officers all over the country. It means that the Boy Scouts are going to be recognized, if we make good, as a sort of reserve supply for the militia. But we are going, if we go, without thinking about that at all. Forget the militia, and remember only that you will have a chance to do real scouting, and to make real reports of a real enemy."

"Look here," cried Dick Crawford, the Assistant Scout-Master, suddenly, "I want everyone to join in and give three cheers for Scout-Master Durland. I know how hard he's worked to give every one of us a chance to make this trip and get the experience of real scouting. And it's up to every one of us to see that he doesn't have any reason to feel sorry that he did it. He trusts us to make good, and we've certainly got to see to it that we do. Come now— three times three for the Scout-Master!"

Then came the formal giving of the instructions that were required for preparation for the trip. Each Scout got word of the equipment that he himself must bring.

"And mind, now, no extras," said Durland, warningly. "If the weather is at all hot, it's going to be hard work carrying all we must carry, and we don't want any Scouts to have to drop out on the march because their knapsacks are too heavy. We will camp by ourselves, and we will keep to ourselves, except when we're on duty. Remember that I, as commander of the Troop, take rank only as a National Guard captain, and that I am subject to the orders of every major and other field officer who may be present.

"Some of the militiamen and their officers may be inclined to play tricks, and to tease us, but the best way to stop them is to pay no attention to them at all. Now, I want every boy to go home and spend the time he can spare before the start studying all the Scout rules, and brushing up his memory on scoutcraft and campcraft. Polish up your drill manual, too. That may be useful. We want to present a good appearance when we get out there with the soldiers."

The start for the camp of the State militia, who were to gather under the command of Brigadier-General Harkness at a small village near the State line, called Guernsey, was to be made on Sunday. The Scouts would be in camp Sunday night, ready at the first notes of the general reveille on Monday morning to turn out and do their part in the work of defending their State against the invasion of the Blue Army, under General Bliss, of the rival State.

"You see," said Jack, explaining matters to Pete Stubbs and Tom Binns as they went home together after the meeting, "we are classed as the Red Army, and we are supposed to be on the defensive. The Blue Army will try to capture the State capital, and it is our business to defeat them if possible."

"How can they tell whether we beat them or not, if we don't do any fighting?" asked Tom Binns.

"In this sort of fighting it's all worked out by theory, just as if it were a game of chess, Tom, and there are umpires to decide every point that comes up."

"How do they decide things, Jack?"

"Why, they ride over the whole scene of operations, either on horseback, or, if the field is very extensive, in automobiles. If troops are surrounded, they are supposed to be captured, and they are sent to the rear, and required to keep out of all the operations that follow. Then the umpires, who are high officers in the regular army, decide according to the positions that are taken which side has the best chance of success. That is, if two brigades, of different sides, line up for action, and get into the best tactical positions possible, the umpires decide which of them would win if they were really engaged in a true war, and the side that gets their decision is supposed to win. The other brigade is beaten, or destroyed, as the case may be."

"Then how about the whole affair?"

"Well, each commanding general works out his strategy, and does his best to bring about a winning position, just as they would at chess, as I said. There is a time limit, you see, and when the time is up the umpires get together, inspect the whole theatre of war, and make their decision."

"It's a regular game, isn't it, Jack?"

"Yes. The Germans call it Krug-spiel—which means war-game, and that term has been adopted all over the world. It's played with maps and pins, too, in the war colleges, both for sea and land, and that's how officers get training for war in time of peace. It isn't an easy game to learn, either."

"Where do we come in, Jack? What is it we're supposed to do?"

"Obey orders, in the first place, absolutely. And I don't know what the orders will be, and neither does anyone else, so I can't tell you just what we'll do.

But, generally speaking, we'll just have to do regular scout duty. It will be up to us to detect the movements of the enemy, and report, through Scout-Master Durland, who'll be Captain Durland, during the maneuvers, to the staff."

"General Harkness's staff, you mean, Jack? Just what is a staff, anyhow?"

"The headquarters staff during a campaign is a sort of extra supply of arms and legs and eyes for the commanding general. The staff officers carry his orders, and represent him in different parts of the field. They carry orders, and receive reports, and they take just as much routine work as possible off the hands of the general, so that he'll be free to make his plans. You see the general never does any actual fighting. He's too valuable to risk his life that way. He's supposed to stay behind, and be ready to take advantage of any chance he sees."

"Times have changed, haven't they, Jack? In the old histories we used to read about generals who led charges and did all sorts of things like that."

"Well, it would be pretty wasteful to put a general in danger that way now, Pete. He's had plenty of chance to prove his bravery, as a rule, and, when he's a general, and has years of experience behind him, the idea is to use his brain. If he is in the rear, and by his eyes and the reports he gets in all sorts of ways, can get a general view of what is going on, he can tell just what is best to be done. Sometimes the only way to win a battle is to sacrifice a whole brigade or a division—to let it be cut to pieces, without a chance to save itself, in order that the rest of the army may have time to change its position, so that the battle can be won. That's the sort of thing the general has got to decide, and if he's in the thick of the fighting in the old-fashioned way, he can't possibly do that."

"I think it's going to be great sport, don't you, Jack?" asked Tom Binns. "Will there be any real firing?"

"Yes—with smokeless powder, because they want to test some new kinds. But they'll use blank cartridges, of course. There'll be just as much noise as ever, but there won't be any danger, of course."

"I don't like the sound of firing much," said Tom Binns, a little shamefacedly. "Even when I know it's perfectly safe and that there aren't any bullets, it makes me awfully nervous."

"This will be good practice for you, then, Tom, because it will help you to get used to it. I hope we'll never have another war, but we want to be ready if we ever do. 'Be prepared'—that's our Scout motto, you know, and it means for the things that we might have to do in war, as well as the regular peaceful things that come up every day."

"Will there be any aeroplanes?" asked Pete Stubbs. "I'm crazy to see one of those things flying sometime, Jack. I never saw one yet, except that time when the fellow landed here and hurt himself. And I didn't see him in the air, but only after he made his landing. The machine was all busted up then, too."

"I think there'll be some aeroplane scouting by the signal corps. Several of the men in that are pretty well off, you know, and they have their own flying machines. I guess that's one of the things they'll try to determine in these maneuvers, the actual, practical usefulness of aeroplanes, and whether biplanes or monoplanes are the best."

"Say, Jack, why couldn't we Boy Scouts build an aeroplane sometime? If we learned something about them this next week, I should think we might be able to do something like that. I know a lot of fellows that have made experiments with toy ones, that wind up with a spring that's made out of rubber bands. They see how far they will fly."

"I think that would be great sport, Pete. But we won't have any time for that until after we've been through the maneuvers. But I'll tell you what some of us may get a chance to do next week, though it's a good deal of a secret yet."

"What's that, Jack! We'll promise not to say a word about it, won't we, Tom?"

"You bet we won't, Jack! Tell us—do!" pleaded Tom Binns.

"I guess it's all right for me to tell you if you won't let it go any further. Well, it's just this. They're going to do a lot of experimenting with a new sort of automobile for scout duty, and I think some of us will get a chance with them."

"Gee, I wish I knew how to run a car the way you do, Jack. I'd love that sort of thing."

"I can soon teach you all I know, Pete. It isn't much. Come on down to the factory garage after work to-morrow morning, and I'll explain the engines to you, instead of eating lunch. Are you on?"

"You bet I am! Will they let us?"

"Mr. Simms will, if I ask him, I'm sure."

CHAPTER II

THE RED ARMY

The Scouts, under Durland and Dick Crawford, went to Guernsey on a special car of a regular train. Durland, in making the arrangements for the trip, had told the adjutant-general of the State militia that he wanted to keep his Troop separate from the regular militiamen, as far as possible.

"I've got an idea, from a few words I've heard dropped," he told that official, "that some of the boys rather resent the idea of the Boy Scouts being included in the maneuvers. So, for the sake of peace, I think perhaps we'd better keep them as far apart as possible. Then, too, I think it will make for better discipline if we stick close together and have our own camp."

"I guess you're right," said the adjutant-general. "I'll give you transportation to Guernsey for your Troop on the noon train on Sunday. There'll be a special car hitched to the train for you. Report to Colonel Henry at Guernsey station, and he'll assign you to camp quarters. You understand—you'll use a military camp, and not your regular Scout camp. The State will provide tents, bedding and utensils, and you will draw rations for your Troop from the commissary department during the maneuvers."

"I understand, Colonel," said Durland. "You know I served in the Spanish war, and I was able to get pretty familiar with conditions."

"I didn't know it, no," said Colonel Roberts, in some surprise. "What command were you with? I didn't get any further than Tampa myself."

"I was on General Shafter's staff in Cuba," said Durland, quietly.

Colonel Roberts looked at the Scout-Master a bit ruefully.

"You're a regular," he said, half-believingly. "Great Scott, you must be a West Pointer!"

"I was," said Durland, with a laugh. "So I guess you'll find that my Troop will understand how to behave itself in camp."

"I surrender!" said the militia colonel, laughing. "If you don't see anything you want, Captain, just ask me for it. You can have anything I've got power to sign orders for. And say—be easy on the boys! They're a bit green, because this active service is something new for most of us. They mean well, but drilling in an armory and actually getting out and getting a taste of field-service conditions are two different things."

"I think it's all splendid training," said Durland, "and if we'd had more of it before the war with Spain there wouldn't have been so many graves filled by the fever. Why, Colonel, it used to make me sick to go around among the volunteer camps about Siboney and see the conditions there, with men who were brave enough to fight the whole Spanish army just inviting fever and all sorts of disease by the rankest sort of carelessness. Their officers were brave gentleman, but, while they might have been good lawyers and doctors and bankers back home, they had never taken the trouble to read the most elementary books on camp life and sanitation. A day's hard reading would have taught them enough to save hundreds of lives. We lost more men by disease than the Spaniards were able to kill at El Caney and San Juan. And it was all needless."

"I'm detached from my regiment for this camp," said Colonel Roberts, earnestly, "but I'm going to get hold of Major Jones as soon as I get to Guernsey, and ask him to have you inspect the Fourteenth and criticize it. Don't hesitate, please, Captain! Just pitch in and tell us what's wrong, and we'll all be eternally grateful to you. And I wish you'd give me a list of those books you were talking about, will you?"

"Gladly," said Durland. "All right, Colonel. I'll have the Troop on hand for that train."

The Scouts enjoyed the trip mightily. Durland took occasion to impress on them some of the differences between a regular Boy Scout encampment and the strict military camp of which, for the next week, they were to form a part.

"Remember to stick close to your own camp," he said. "After taps don't go out of your own company street. There's no need of it, and I don't want any visiting around among the other troops. In a place like this camp, boys and men don't mix very well, and you'd better stick by yourselves. We won't be there very long, anyway, because we'll probably be detached from headquarters Monday. The army will break up, too, because this is really only a concentration camp, where the army will be mobilized."

"When does the war begin?" asked Dick Crawford.

"War is supposed to be declared at noon to-morrow," said Durland. "It is regarded as inevitable already, however, and General Harkness can begin throwing out his troops as soon as he has them ready, though not a shot can be fired before noon. Neither can a single Red or Blue soldier cross the State line before that time. However, I suspect that the line will be pretty well patrolled before the actual declaration, so as to prevent General Bliss from throwing any considerable force across the line before we are ready to meet it. If he could get between Guernsey and the State capital in any force, the chances are that we'd be beaten before we ever began to fight at all."

"That wouldn't do," said Dick Crawford. "Will we have any fortifications to defend at all, sir?"

"Not unless we're driven back pretty well toward the capital. Of course there are no real fortifications there, but imaginary lines have been established there. However, if we were forced to take to those the moral victory would be with the Blues, even though they couldn't actually compel the surrender of the city within the time limit. If I were General Harkness, I think I would try at once to deceive the enemy by presenting a show of strength on his front and carry the war into his own territory by a concealed flanking movement, and if that were properly covered I think we could get between him and his base and cut him off from his supplies."

"You mean you'd really take the offensive as the best means of defense?"

"That's been the principle upon which the best generals always have worked, from Hannibal to Kuroki," said Durland, his eyes lighting up. "Look at the Japanese in their war with Russia. They didn't wait for the Russians to advance through Manchuria. They crossed the border at once, though nine critics out of every ten who had studied the situation expected them to wait for the Russians to cross the Yalu and make Korea the great theater of the war. Instead of that they advanced themselves, beat a small Russian army at the Yalu, and pressed on. They met the Russians, who were pouring into Manchuria over their great Trans-Siberian railway, and drove them back, from Liao Yiang to Mukden. They'd have kept on, too, if they hadn't been stopped by peace."

"Could they have kept on, though? I always had an idea that they needed the peace even more than the Russians did."

"Well, you may be right. That's something that no one can tell. They had the confidence of practically unceasing victory from the very beginning of the war. They were safe from invasion, because their fleet absolutely controlled the Yellow Sea after the battle of Tsushima, and there weren't any more Russian battleships to bother them. They had bottled up the Russian force in Port Arthur, and they were in the position of having everything to gain and very little to lose. Their line of communication was perfectly safe."

"They must have weakened themselves greatly, though, in that series of battles."

"Yes, they did. And, of course, there is the record of Russia to be considered. Russia has always been beaten at the start of a war. It has taken months of defeat to stiffen the Russians to a real fight. Napoleon marched to Moscow fairly easily, though he did have some hard fights, like the one at Borodino, on the way. But he had a dreadful time getting back, and that was what destroyed him. After that Leipzic and Waterloo were inevitable. It was the Russians who really won the fight against Napoleon, though it remained for Blucher and Wellington to strike the death blows."

"Well, after all, what might have happened doesn't count for so much. It's what did really happen that stands in history, and the Japanese won. It was by their daring in taking the offensive and striking quickly that they did that, you think?"

"It certainly seems so to me! And look at the Germans in the war with France. Von Moltke decided that the thing to do was to strike at the very heart and soul of France—Paris. So he swept on, leaving great, uncaptured fortresses like Metz and Sedan behind him, which was against every rule of war as it was understood then. Of course, Metz and Sedan were both captured, but it was daring strategy on the part of Von Moltke. It was supposed then to be suicidal for an army to pass by a strong fortress, even if it were invested."

"That was how the Boers made so much trouble for the English, too, wasn't it?"

"Certainly it was. The English expected the Boers to sit back and wait to be attacked. Instead of that the Boers swept down at once on both sides of the continent, and besieged Kimberly and Ladysmith. That was how they were able to prolong the war. They took the offensive, in spite of being outnumbered, and while they could never have really hoped to win, they put up a wonderful fight."

"Well, I suppose we'll know in a day or so what General Harkness plans to do."

"Hardly! We're not connected with the staff in any way, and he'll discuss his plans only with his own staff officers. He has an excellent reputation. He commanded a brigade in the Porto Rico campaign, you know, and did very well, though that campaign was a good deal of a joke. But one reason that it was a joke was that it was so well planned by General Miles and the others under him that there was no use, at any stage of it, in a real resistance on the part of the Spaniards. They were beaten before a shot was fired, and they had sense enough not to waste lives uselessly."

"Then they weren't cowardly?"

"No, indeed, and don't let anyone tell you they were, either. The Spaniards were a brave and determined enemy, but they were so crippled and hampered by orders from home that they were unable to make much of a showing in the field. We'll learn some time, I'm afraid, that we won that war too easily. Overconfidence is our worst national fault. Just because we never have been beaten, we think we're invincible. I hope the lesson, when it does come, and if it does come, won't be too costly."

The run to Guernsey was not a very long one. The train arrived there at four o'clock in the afternoon, and the Scouts, armed only with their clasp knives,

Scout axes and sticks, lined up on the platform in excellent order. Dick Crawford, who ranked as a lieutenant for the encampment, took command, while Durland reported the arrival to Colonel Henry, as he had been ordered to do.

Half a dozen extra sidings had been laid for the occasion by the railroad, and on these long trains, each carrying militia, had been shunted. Clad all in khaki, or, rather, in the substitute adopted by the American army as more serviceable and less easy to distinguish at a distance, a stout cloth of olive drab, thousands of sturdy militiamen were standing at ease, waiting for orders to move. Field guns, too, and horses, for the mounted troops, were being unloaded, and the scene was one of the greatest activity. Hoarse cries filled the air, but there was only the appearance of confusion, since the citizen soldiers understood their work thoroughly, and each man had his part to play in the spectacle.

From one of the trains, too, three great structures with spreading wings had been unloaded, and the eyes of the Boy Scouts turned constantly toward the spot where mechanics were busily engaged in assembling the aeroplanes which were to serve, to some extent, as the eyes of the army.

"Glad to see you, Captain," Colonel Henry said to Durland when the Scout-Master reported the arrival of his Troop. "I'll send an orderly with you to show you the location of your camp. Colonel Roberts directed me to give you an isolated location, and I have done so. It's a little way from drinking water, but I guess you won't mind that."

"Not a bit, sir," said Durland, smilingly.

"Very well, Captain. Report to General Harkness's tent at eight o'clock, sir, for your instructions. I think you will find that the General has enough work planned to keep your Troop pretty busy to-morrow. We shall all watch your work with a great deal of interest. We've been hearing a lot about Durland's Scouts."

Durland saluted then, and turned with the orderly to rejoin his Troop.

In two hours the camp was ready. The neat row of tents, making a short but perfectly planned and arranged company street, were all up, bedding was ready, and supper was being cooked from the rations supplied by the commissary department. Durland, with active recollections of commissary supplies, had been inclined to bring along extra supplies for his Troop, but had decided against doing so, though he knew that many of the militia companies had taken the opposite course to his own, and had brought along enough supplies to set an excellent table.

"I want the boys to get a taste of real service," he told Dick, "and it won't hurt them a bit to rough it for a week. They get enough to eat, even if there isn't much variety, and the quality isn't of the best. The stuff is wholesome, anyhow—that's what counts."

By the time he returned from headquarters, the Troop was sound asleep, save for the sentries, Tom Binns and Harry French, who challenged him briskly.

CHAPTER III

THE SCOUTING AUTO

Reveille sounded at five o'clock. There was plenty to be done before the war game actually began. There were plans to be laid, codes to be determined, umpires to be consulted as to vague and indefinite rules, and all sorts of little things that in a real war would have adjusted themselves. But the Scouts were well out of the excitement. They struck their tents and handed them over, neatly arranged, with all their bedding, to the men from the commissary department.

"Sleeping bags for us, after to-day," explained Durland. "That is, if we have to sleep in the open. Sometimes we'll get a barn or a hayrick, or even a bed in a farmhouse. We won't worry about all that. But we're not going to sit still, and we can't scout and carry tents and dunnage of that sort along. So I said I'd turn it all in."

Then the Troop waited, quietly, for the orders that seemed so slow in coming. But they came at last. A young officer rode up on a horse that was dripping wet.

"General Harkness's compliments, Captain," he said, saluting Durland, "and you will take your Troop at once to Bremerton, on the State line. You will make your headquarters there, where a field telegraph station has been established. Please hold your Scouts for the stroke of twelve, when they may cross the line. The line for five miles on each side of Bremerton is in your territory."

"My compliments to General Harkness, and we will start at once," replied Durland.

And a moment later they were on the hike. There was plenty of time, since Bremerton was less than three miles away, and it was scarcely seven o'clock, but it was cooler then than it would be later, and Durland was glad to get his Troop away from the bustle and apparent confusion of the camp where the Red army was beginning to move.

"Where are the divisional headquarters to be to-day?" Durland asked a hurrying staff officer who passed just then.

"Hardport—across the line," the staff man replied, as he paused a moment. A wide grin illuminated his features. "That's nerve for you, eh? The old man's pretty foxy. He's going to start us moving so that we'll begin crossing the State line on the stroke of twelve, and he'll fling a brigade into Hardport before two o'clock."

Durland whistled.

"That's fine, if it works," he remarked to Dick Crawford, later. "But Hardport practically is the key to the railroad situation, and it isn't conceivable that the Blues will leave it unguarded. I'm inclined to be a wee bit dubious about that."

However, as he reflected, it was really none of his business. He was responsible for his own Troop, not for the conduct of the campaign, and that let him out.

It was a hot, hazy day, when the sun was fully up, and the Scouts marched into Bremerton, to find it a sleepy, lazy, old-fashioned little town. Above a building in the center the national flag was floating, and next to it a Red standard. Durland turned the Troop over to Dick Crawford, with instructions to make a bivouac near the centre of the little place, and then walked over to the building where the flag was flying.

As he surmised, it had become unexpectedly brigade headquarters for the fourth brigade of the Red army, which had left Guernsey before the breakfast call had been sounded for most of the army, and had arrived too soon.

"Where is your brigade, Tomlinson?" he asked a young officer, who almost ran into him as he came out.

"Oh, hello, Durland!" said the officer, wheeling briskly to shake hands with the Scout-Master. "Why, we're hidden in the woods. Old Beansy's fuming and fretting because he's here too soon. The men are lying back there, but he's moved up here for brigade headquarters because it's a field telegraph station and he can talk as much as he likes with General Harkness."

"Your brigade commander is Beansy, I take it?" said Durland, with a grin.

"You're right, he is! General Beverly Bean, bless him! He'll want to see you, too, now that you've blundered into his territory. Go on up—third door to the left!"

Durland stopped to report his arrival to division headquarters and then went on, getting into the presence of General Bean after a few minutes' delay.

"Glad to see you sir," said the testy old officer, who was a real soldier. "Suppose you know we're intended to get into Hardport just as soon after this war begins as we can get there."

"How soon will that be?" asked Durland.

"About two hours, if we're not cut to pieces on the way. I want your help here, Captain. Can you send some of your Scouts over there to investigate? I've an idea that getting into Hardport may be easier than getting out again.

If Bliss knows his business, he will be regarding that as a pretty important place."

"I've orders to cover five miles each side of Bremerton," said Durland. "I can spare two Scouts for any duty you may wish done, General. Could they have a car?"

"Do they know how to run one?"

The question was asked in evident surprise, but Durland replied confidently.

"Yes, General," said he. "I've got two Scouts, at least, who are perfectly capable of handling an automobile under any conditions. I'd trust myself to them, no matter how hard the road might be."

"I'm glad to hear it," said the general, rather dryly. "I've got two of those new-fangled scout duty cars, with an armored hood and those new non-explosive tires, that can't be stopped by a bullet aimed at the wheels. But they didn't send me anyone to run them. There may be some chauffeurs in my brigade, but I'm not too anxious to take any men from their regiments. Here—I'll give you an order for one of the cars. Let your Scouts make the best use they can of it."

Durland had heard of the new scouting cars, but had never seen one. He went now, since there was plenty of time, to look it over, and found a heavy but high-powered and fast machine of a most unusual type.

The hood was armored, so that no stray bullets could reach the engine, as would be easy enough in the ordinary car. Similar protection was afforded to the big gasoline tank in the rear of the car, and the seats, intended for two men, were covered by a shield, also of bullet-proof armor, that was so pierced with small holes that the road ahead could be seen.

But the most extraordinary feature of the car was the new type of wheel. There were no tires in the ordinary sense at all. Instead, there was a tough, but springy steel substitute, and Durland spent an hour in looking the queer contrivance over, having first satisfied himself that the car was not sufficiently different from the ordinary automobile to make it impossible for Jack Danby to operate it. For it was Jack Danby he had had in mind when he asked for the use of the machine.

His friend Lieutenant Tomlinson came up while he was looking it over.

"Queer lookin' critter, isn't it?" said Tomlinson. He seemed quite enthusiastic. "I tell you what," he went on, "if that thing works out all right, it's going to revolutionize certain things in warfare. And it's perfect, theoretically. Tires are the things that have barred automobiles from use in warfare so far. Ping!—a bullet hits a tire, and the car is stalled. Or suppose the chauffeur wants to leave the road and go 'cross country? His tires again. He's afraid to."

"And this has tires that won't be afraid of bullets or rocks, either, eh?"

"I should say they wouldn't! Bullets wouldn't have a chance against that stuff. And the man who drives it is protected, too. That bullet-proof shield makes him as safe as if he were at home. And the blooming thing is good for sixty miles an hour over a half-way decent road—though it can be slowed down to just about two miles an hour, and still be ready for a quick jump."

"They're being used in both armies, aren't they?"

"Yes. There are about a dozen of them altogether. They're evenly divided, and both armies are under orders to try them out pretty thoroughly. If they make good, there will be a lot of them put in use by the regular army. They're making their own tests, but tests under actual service conditions count for more than any number of trials when all the conditions are made to order for the people who are trying to put the cars over."

It was Tomlinson's busy day, and he didn't have time to dally long in talk. So he went off, and Durland sent Tom Binns, who was acting as his orderly for the day, to bring Jack Danby to him.

Durland carried in his pockets a number of large scale maps of the sections all around the State line, in both of the States. The scale was two inches to the mile, so it took a considerable number of the maps to show at all adequately the theatre of the imaginary war. But so full of detail, thanks to the large scale, were the maps, that they showed every house in the territory they covered, and every grade. He spread three of these maps out, side by side, as he waited for Jack, and traced a course over them with a pencil.

Jack appeared in due time, and saluted—not with the Scout salute of thumb and little finger bent, with the three other fingers held straight up, but with the military salute.

"Danby," said Durland, "I'm going to entrust you with a piece of work that is so important that the whole result of the maneuvers may depend upon it. Do you think you can run that car?"

Jack, who had a positive genius for mechanical matters of all sorts, looked the strange looking car over carefully before he answered.

"It looks straight enough, sir," he said. "Self starter, I guess. And you ought to be able to go anywhere you like with those wheels. What is it that I am to do, sir?"

"I can explain better with these maps," said Durland. "Come close here, and I will show you what I mean."

Jack bent over the maps with the Scout-Master, and Durland began tracing a line with a sharp pencil.

"Here we are, in Bremerton," he said. "Now, about four miles across the State line is Hardport. You can see the smoke from its factories, and the railroad yards there, because it's quite an important little city. Now, there is a straight road from here that leads there—the continuation of this very road we are on now. What I want you to do is to circle around"—he pointed on the map—"and strike into Hardport from the other side. Find out, if possible, what troops of the Blue army are in the neighborhood, and particularly along this main road. If they occupy it in force, report as quickly as possible. If they advance immediately after war is declared, return, but try to see if there is not some way in which our own troops can get behind them."

"Am I to go into Hardport itself, sir?"

"Yes. And you need not stop, if challenged. Your car is regarded as bullet proof, and the only way in which they can legitimately capture you is by stretching a rope or providing some sort of an obstruction that enables two of them to get a foot on your running board. Remember your rights, and don't surrender to a mere challenge from a sentry. And keep your hood well down, so that they won't recognize you."

"I understand, sir. What time am I to start from here?"

"Start as soon as you like. You'd better get off and circle pretty widely, so as to get used to the car. But don't cross the State line, whatever you do, before twelve o'clock. That is strictly against orders."

There was a lot of good-natured talk among the Scouts when they heard of the great chance to distinguish himself that had come to the Assistant Patrol Leader of the Crows.

"Gee, Jack's lucky!" said one member of the Whip-poor-will Patrol.

"He is not!" defended Pete Stubbs, loyally. "He's a hard worker. He's spent a lot of his own time in the last year learnin' all about an automobile. He knows how to run one, and he knows how to fix it, too, if it goes wrong on a trip. That isn't luck, and don't you call it luck!"

"I didn't mean anything against Jack when I said he was lucky, Pete. No call to get so mad about it!"

"I'm not so mad, but it does get my goat to hear people say that everything that happens to Jack Danby that's good comes because he's lucky. I guess he isn't any luckier than any of the rest of us, but he sticks to the job harder."

No amount of coaxing, of course, would have induced Jack to tell what his orders were; and as a matter of fact, only one or two of the Scouts tried to find out. Durland had not even thought it necessary to warn Jack to be quiet, for he knew that Jack was on his honor as a Scout, and that nothing more was necessary to lead him to maintain a resolute silence on the subject of the strange scouting trip into the enemy's country which he was soon to begin.

"Good luck," cried the Scout-Master, finally, as Jack started off. "You know your orders—now make good!"

CHAPTER IV

IN THE ENEMY'S COUNTRY

Almost at the last moment Scout-Master Durland, or Captain Durland, as he was again for this week, had decided not to send Jack Danby on his trip into the enemy's country alone. Seated beside Jack, therefore, under the protective hood of the scout car, was little Tom Binns.

"Keep your eye on your watch, Tom," said Jack. "We don't want to make any mistake and cross the line too soon—but we don't want to be late, either. This job is too important to run any risks of bungling it. I'd hate to think that I'd been trusted with something really big for the first time and then fallen down on it."

"Where will you cross the line, Jack?" asked Tom. "I should think it would be pretty hard to tell just where the boundary was."

Jack pointed to a road map, on a slightly smaller scale than the one from which Captain Durland had given him his course, which was pasted right before his eyes on the metal dashboard of the car.

"I can't lose my way with that, Tom," he said. "See, there's a road that we're getting pretty near to now. It crosses the State line about six miles east of Bremerton, if you'll notice the map, at a little village called Mardean. That's all on this side of the line. They may be watching the road there, so what we want to do is to get where we can't be seen, and then, about a minute before noon, go ahead as fast as the car will carry us. That ought to take us through all right, even if they've got a guard on duty. Then we can circle around in a big sweep and come down to Hardport from behind. The country people ought to be able to tell us part of what we want to know, and we can confirm what they tell us by what we can see ourselves."

"They wouldn't lie to us, would they, Jack?"

"You couldn't call it regular lying if they gave us false information about their own army, Tom. Remember that this is supposed to be like a real war, and in a war the invading army wouldn't expect to get correct information from the people along the roads. On the contrary, they'd do their best to delay the enemy, and make all the trouble they could, and they'd be patriotic. So we've got to be mighty careful this next week about how we take any information we pick up in that fashion. If the people on the farms take the game seriously, and enter into the spirit of it, they'll do all they can to harass us and bother us."

Jack drove his car well and carefully, but made no great attempt to get high speed out of it, though it was, as he knew, capable of going three or four times as fast as he was driving it. But there is always a certain danger in driving an automobile at high speed, and Jack saw no use in taking any risk that was not necessary.

"You can go a lot faster than this, can't you, Jack?" asked Tom, as they bowled along easily, at little more than fifteen miles an hour.

"What's the use, Tom? We'll get to Mardean before we can cross the line, anyhow. I'll go fast enough then for a spell, if you're anxious for speed. Don't be impatient! We'll get all the speed you want before very long."

Jack was a true prophet, as one ought to be when he has the means of fulfilling the prophecy in his own hands. At Mardean, just out of sight of the line, they waited while the minutes dragged slowly by.

"One minute more!" cried Tom Binns, breathless with excitement and suspense.

"All right," said Jack, quietly. "Hold tight now, Tom! I'm going to let her out a bit."

Swiftly the grey car gathered speed. In a rush of dust, with horn blowing and exhaust sputtering behind them, the car shot over the line, and, just as a whistle boomed out the twelve o'clock dinner signal, Jack was in hostile territory. The war was on!

Behind them there was a confused shouting. The car was built so that it was easy to look behind.

"There was an outpost there," said Tom, as he looked back. "They're kicking up a tremendous fuss, Jack. I guess we rather put one over on them that time."

"We've got to put another one over on them in a hurry, then," said Jack, "or they'll put one over on us. Let me know as soon as that outpost is well out of sight, Tom. And keep your eyes skinned for any sign that they're after us with a motorcycle or anything like that, will you?"

"They're out of sight now—and there's nothing on the road. Hey, Jack, where are you going?"

For Jack, after a swift glance at his map, had run deliberately off the road, reducing speed considerably as he did so, but not so much that the car did not rattle around considerably as it left the smooth roadbed and plunged into a field that had not long since been ploughed.

"They'll telephone ahead of us, and they'll be waiting," Jack explained. "I've got to cut through the fields here, so that we can get on another road where they won't be looking for us. Otherwise I'm afraid we wouldn't get very far before we ran into a trap that all our armor and all our speed wouldn't get us out of without capture. You don't want to lose this car on its first trip, do you, Tom?"

"Not by a good deal!" yelled Tom, who was beginning to feel the exhilaration of the wild, bumping ride over the furrows of the field. "It was sort of sudden, that's all, Jack; I wasn't expecting it, you see."

"I meant to tell you we'd do that, but I forgot. I had it all doped out. See, we're coming to another road, now. This is a pretty big field, and it was marked accurately on that map. This whole section was surveyed and mapped especially for this war game."

"Say, if they do many things like that, it must cost something," said Tom.

"War's the most expensive thing in the world, Tom, and the next most expensive, I guess, is getting ready for it, and having such a strong army and navy that no one will want to fight you. But it pays to be ready for war, no matter how much it costs, for the country that isn't ready is always the one that has to fight when it least expects it. And fighting when you're not ready is the most expensive of all. It costs money and lives."

Then, with a sickening bump, the car took the road again, and Jack was heading straight for Hardport.

"Those wheels worked splendidly," he said. "And the car, too. An ordinary car would have bumped itself to pieces a mile or so back, and this one is running just as easily as when we started. I suppose it cost a lot, but it was certainly worth it."

"Every time we hit a new furrow I thought we were going to break down," confessed Tom. "I was scared at first. But I soon decided that we were all right. But I don't believe, even if I knew how to drive a car, that I'd have the nerve to take it through a ploughed field that way."

"Yes, you would, Tom, if you knew it was the only thing you could do. You couldn't be any worse scared than I was when we left the road—but I knew, you see, that there simply wasn't any other way out of it. When you have to do a thing, you can usually manage it. I've found that out."

"What's next?"

"The outskirts of Hardport. I want to skirt the railroad track. Their mobilization was at Smithville, back along the railroad about twenty miles, and if they've sent any force to Hardport, the railroad will show it. If they haven't, I'm going to mark the railroad cut."

"What do you mean, Jack?"

"In a real war, if people got a chance, this railroad would be cut. A lot of rails would be torn up and burnt. We don't want to interfere with regular traffic, so in this game we build a fire with spare ties, and mark as much rail as we'd have time to tear up, allowing ten minutes for each length of rail. Then if a troop train comes along and sees that signal, it is held to be delayed an hour for each torn up rail, as that is the time it would take the sappers to repair the damage."

They paused for thirty minutes, therefore, when they reached a spot about three miles and a half from the city line of Hardport.

"There," said Jack, when he had set his marks, "that will hold them up for three hours, and give General Bean a chance to occupy Hardport and destroy the railroad bridge. That will take a day to rebuild, without interference, and I guess it makes it pretty safe for us. Now we'll go on into town."

But they didn't go into the town. They did not have to, to discover that Hardport was occupied by a Blue regiment, which had outposts well scattered around the place, anticipating an attack, just as Captain Durland had said he thought would be the case.

"We'll do some more circling, now," said Jack, "and get around their outposts. I know a way we can do that. What they're planning is to let General Bean advance and walk into a trap. They've got enough men waiting for him along here to smash him on a frontal attack. What we've got to do is to get word to him in time to prevent him from doing that."

Twice, as the grey car sped along, now on the road, now in the fields, they saw parties of the enemy, but never were they near enough seriously to threaten the Boy Scouts with capture. And at last, striking into the main road for Bremerton, they saw a cloud of dust approaching, which they recognized as the signal of the coming of General Bean's brigade.

The soldiers cheered them as they recognized the scout car, and opened up a way for the big car to pass through them to the brigade commander himself.

"What's your name, eh?" asked the General, sharply. "Danby, eh? Excellent work, Scout Danby! I shall make it a point to report my appreciation to your Troop commander. You'd better come along in the rear now, and watch the rest of the operations. Thanks to you, I rather think they'll be worth watching."

And, touching the spurs to his speedy black horse, he cantered up to the front of the column, chuckling and laughing as he thought of how the enemy had been outwitted by his youthful Scout.

The direct forward march of the brigade was interrupted immediately. One regiment, indeed, continued along the straight road to Hardport, but the rest of the brigade was deployed at once.

"What will they do now, Jack?" asked Tom Binns.

"Well, I wouldn't be able to say for certain," replied Jack, with a smile, "but I rather think they'll manage to get behind the town in some fashion, and close in on the Blue troops in the garrison while the regiment in front here keeps them busy with a strong feint of an attack."

A colonel of regular cavalry, with a white badge on his arm to show he was serving as an umpire, drove past just then in a big white automobile.

"See, there's one of the umpires," said Jack. "He goes all about, and determines the result. I'm glad he's here—that means there can't be any dispute this time. General Bean has probably told him what he plans to do, and he will see how it comes out. Of course, he doesn't communicate in any way with the enemy, or tell them what we're planning to do."

"Of course not! That wouldn't be fair, Jack. I'm glad he's here, too. Do you suppose he's heard about the way we blocked the railroad?"

"I think he may have seen our signs and come this way just to find out what was doing."

"Listen!" cried Jack, suddenly. "There's firing ahead! Let's get on and find out what's going on."

There was heavy firing ahead of them for a few minutes, and then it became intermittent.

"Our attack is being repelled, I guess," said Jack. "That's the first engagement of the war, too. Well, we may seem to be beaten in that, but I guess we can afford to lose a skirmish, if we can capture Hardport and a whole Blue regiment."

Again, after the firing had almost ceased, a rattle of shots burst on the quiet air. Then, too, came the screaming of a shell, as it burst harmlessly above the city.

"Hooray!" cried Jack. "We've surrounded them! Come on!"

And this time there was no opposing the entry of the grey car into Hardport. The city had been surrounded and captured, just as Jack had predicted, and the Blue regiment that had been so completely outwitted, thanks to the cleverness of Jack Danby, was out of the war entirely. It was an important victory, in more ways than one. General Bliss could ill afford to lose so many men, and the capture of Hardport, moreover, was a crippling blow, since it interfered with the operation of the railroad which he had relied upon for bringing his troops across the State line in large numbers.

The umpires lost no time in telling General Bean of their decision, and in congratulating him on the strategy he had displayed.

"Cutting the railroad was a masterly stroke," said one of the umpires.

"That's what I say!" said the General, with enthusiasm. "And it was a little tike of a Boy Scout, in my grey scout car, who did it—and that without orders!"

CHAPTER V

OFF TO CRIPPLE CREEK

Jack and Tom Binns waited only to see the surrender of Hardport before Jack turned the car about and made for Bremerton, taking the direct road this time, since the advance of General Bean and his division of the Red army had swept aside all danger from the invading Blue forces. The outposts, of course, which Jack had had to dodge as he scouted in advance of the Red advance guard, had all been driven back upon Hardport, and they were prisoners of war now, and the way was clear for the day, at least.

Captain Durland listened with scarcely concealed enthusiasm to Jack's clear and concise account of what had been accomplished.

"You two saved the day," he said, finally. "We would have been in a very tight hole indeed if you hadn't cut the railroad, which was the only thing that made it possible for General Bean to effect the capture of Hardport as he did."

"How is that, sir?" asked Jack. "I thought we gave him useful information, and I cut the railroad because there seemed to be a good chance to do it, without thinking very much of the consequences of doing so."

"Why, if you hadn't cut the railroad," said Durland, "General Bliss would have thrown a division into Hardport as soon as he heard at his headquarters, by telegraph, that the place was threatened. Then he could have moved troops over from Mardean, where I imagine he had at least a couple of regiments, and General Bean's brigade would have been in a trap that would have been absolutely impossible to escape from. Now it's all different. We've got Hardport. By this time General Bean has unquestionably theoretically destroyed the railroad bridge and has artillery mounted so that the guns will have to be captured before General Bliss can make an attempt to rebuild it."

"I see! If the bridge is covered with guns, the theory is that the enemy couldn't do any work, eh?"

"Exactly! They've got to work in a narrow place, and they'd be blown to pieces, a squad at a time, while they were trying to work. That was the decisive move of the whole action. What did General Bean say to you?"

"He said it was good work, sir, and that he was going to speak to you of it."

"Excellent, Jack! I am very pleased that one of my Scouts should have played so important a part in the first decisive engagement of the campaign. And General Bean is the sort of a man who is sure to see that you get the credit for what you've done."

"What shall we do next, sir?"

"I'll hold you in reserve until I get further orders from headquarters, I think. General Harkness evidently plans an aggressive fight from the very outset. I have heard nothing from his headquarters direct as yet, but I probably shall pretty soon. I shall send in a report of General Bean's success at Hardport at once, though he has probably done that already."

The Scouts were working well all along the line. The enemy, as Pete Stubbs had reported, had crossed the State line in some small force at Mardean. Two regiments had occupied that village, which was on the Red side of the line, and had thrown out skirmishers for a couple of miles in both directions. Warner, one of the Raccoon Patrol, had been captured, but he was the only one of the Troop who had not made good his escape in the face of the enemy's advance, and even he had accomplished the purpose for which he had been sent out, since he had managed to wig-wag the news of the advance of a troop of cavalry before they had run him down, and the news had been flashed all along the line, from Scout to Scout, until it had reached Durland.

The wireless was not in use here, though experiments were being made with a field wireless installation some miles away, but the Scouts did not need it. They were spread out within plain sight of one another, and with their little red and white flags they sent messages by the Morse alphabet, and in a special code, as fast as wireless could have done. They also were prepared to use, when there was a bright sun, which was not the case that day, the heliograph system, which sends messages for great distances.

In that system of field signalling, extensively employed by the British during the Boer war, since wireless had not at that time been at all perfected, a man stands on a slight elevation, and catches the rays of the sun on a great reflector. Those flashes are visible for many miles in a clear atmosphere, in a flat country, and the flashes, of course, are practically instantaneous.

"We don't need to worry about wireless for communications of a few miles," said Durland. "The system of signalling that depends on seeing flashes, smokes, flags and other signals, is as old as warfare, really. The Indians, in this country, used to send news an astonishing distance in an amazingly short time. They used smokes, as we know, since we have all worked out those signals ourselves from time to time. And all nations in time of war have employed relays of men with flags, stationed at fixed intervals for scores of miles, for the sending of despatches and important news. Napoleon used the system on a great scale, and, until the telegraph was invented and made practicable for field work, that was the only way it could be done."

"The telegraph was first used in our Civil War, wasn't it, sir?" asked Tom Binns.

"Yes. But even then it was done in a very crude way. There was none of the modern elaborate work of field telegraph systems. Nowadays, you see, an army builds its telegraph lines as it goes along. Then they were dependent upon the lines already built, mostly along the railroad tracks. The first really great war in which such systems were in use was the struggle between Russia and Japan. The French and the Germans didn't have them in their war."

A few minutes later an orderly from the building in which the field telegraph station had been established came running up to Durland.

"Despatch from General Harkness, Captain," he said, saluting, and Durland took the slip of paper. He flushed with pleasure as he read it.

"Concentrate your troop at Hardport," he read. "Send Danby and companion in scout car ahead, to report to me for special duty. Congratulations on his splendid work, reported to me fully by General Bean."

"That is the sort of thing that makes it worth while to do good work," he said. "I think we saved General Harkness from an embarrassing position this morning, and it is good to think that he appreciates what we were able to do. Get along, now, Jack, and report to headquarters just as soon as you can."

There was now no need to take the grey car through the fields as Jack retraced their course over the straight road from Bremerton. They met pickets, but those they met, who had heard something of the deeds Jack had already accomplished, cheered his progress now, since this was no longer the enemy's country but a part of Red territory, by virtue of Bean's swift and successful attack of the morning. The soldiers they saw were a part of their own army, and Jack waved his hand in grateful acknowledgment of the cheers that pursued them as they sped by.

"Those fellows are regulars," he told Tom, as they passed one small detachment. "It makes you feel good to think that they regard us as comrades in arms, doesn't it, Tom? Those fellows know what they're about, and they must regard some of our militia as a good deal of a joke."

"I don't think that's a bit fair, Jack," said Tom. "The militia have their own work to do most of the time, and they do the best they can when they turn soldiers. And if we had a war, the regulars wouldn't be able to go very far without help—they must know that!"

"They're not mean about it, Tom. They help the militia as much as they can when they're in camp together, and teach them the tricks of the trade. But they're trained men who don't do anything but work at their soldiering, and the trained men always feel a bit superior to the volunteers."

"Some countries have a much bigger army than we do, don't they, Jack?"

"Indeed they do! Why, in Europe, in every country except England, every man has to serve in the army, unless he's too weak to do it. You see, they have possible enemies on all sides of them. Over here we don't realize how lucky we are to have the sea guarding us from the most dangerous enemies we might have. We haven't any reason to fear trouble with England, and Canada, of course, isn't any better off than we when it comes to an army.

We could take care of them easily enough with the trained troops we have. And Mexico, while they might fight us, couldn't put up any sort of a real fight. The Mexicans couldn't invade this country, and if we ever had to invade Mexico, we'd have all the time we needed to train an army to go across and fight them, the way we did before. We may have to do that some time, but I hope not, because fighting in the sort of country there is down there would mean an awful loss of life."

"You mean that they know the country so well that a small force of them could worry us and make a lot of trouble, even if we won all the big battles?"

"Yes. The Boers couldn't stand up to the British very long in their fight, but they kept under arms and made the English armies work mighty hard to bring about peace."

"Well, I hope we never do have a war, Jack. This is only a game, of course, but it gives you an idea of what the real thing would be like, and it must be dreadful. It makes me realize, somehow, what it might have been like in the Civil War, when we were killing one another. Somehow reading about those battles doesn't give you as much of an idea of how it must have been as even a single morning of this sham war."

They were moving along fast as they talked, and they were in the outskirts of Hardport now. The town was full of soldiers. General Bean's brigade had been reinforced by the arrival of nearly ten thousand more men, and there were, altogether, about sixteen thousand troops there. General Harkness, thanks to Jack Danby and the quick wit of General Bean, who had understood the necessity of altering his plans for the capture of the place when he got Jack's report, had made good his boast that he would make the place his divisional headquarters for the night.

The place was all astir. Small automobiles, painted red, carried bustling officers from place to place, delivering orders, preparing for the next step in the defense of the State capital. General Harkness, Jack found, after making several fruitless inquiries of officers who seemed to be too busy to bother with a small boy, who, had they known it, was a far more important factor in the campaign than they were at all likely to be, had established his headquarters at the Hardport House, the leading hotel of the town, and there Jack went.

He was kept waiting for some time, after he had stated his name, and that he was under orders to report to the commanding general, but when he reached General Harkness he found him a pleasant, courteous man, and very much pleased with the work that he and Tom Binns had done.

"Now," said the General, "I've got some more and very important work for you to do. I've got to find out as soon as I can what the enemy's plans are. I don't expect you to do all of that, but you can play a part."

He walked over to a great wall map of the whole field of the operations, and pointed out a road on it.

"That road is the key to the situation this afternoon," he said. "General Bean is pressing forward to reach it as soon as possible, and occupy this bridge here in force. If he can get there in time, the enemy's advance will be checked. It is likely, in fact, that we may be able to force a decisive engagement there before the enemy is at all ready for it. Our capture of Hardport to-day, you see, has given us a great advantage. Before that, the enemy was in a position to choose his fighting ground. He could make us meet him where he liked, and with all the advantage of position in his favor. Now that will be no longer possible for him. The ground at Cripple Creek Bridge here is the best we could have, since, if General Bean can occupy the position there, General Bliss will have no choice but to give battle there, and I think we can turn him back on his own mobilization point."

Jack saluted.

"I am to report on the number and disposition of the enemy's forces about Cripple Creek, then, sir?" he said.

"Those are your orders. I shall expect a report within two hours."

"Yes, General. I will do my best to have one within that time."

Off in the distance, as Jack whirled out of Hardport, and beyond the last pickets of the Red army, he saw a cloud of dust spreading across the country.

"There's General Bean," he said to Tom. "Gee, his fellows must be pretty tired! They've fought a battle and captured a town already, and now they're off on a fifteen-mile march. Going some, I think!"

Cripple Creek was fifteen miles by the straight route the troops were forced to take, but by short cuts and taking bad roads, Jack could reach it by less than nine miles of traveling.

"Keep your eyes skinned, Tom!" said Jack, as he drove along. "I've got to watch the road, and we're in the enemy's country again with a vengeance."

CHAPTER VI

AT THE COVERED BRIDGE

There was not a sign of the enemy as they neared the bridge, one of those covered affairs so common a few years ago in country districts. The countryside was serene and undisturbed.

"This doesn't look much like war," said Jack. "But I guess Gettysburg itself looked just as peaceful a few days before the big battle in 1863. You can't always tell by appearances. We'll go pretty easy here, anyhow, until we're certain that it's all right."

But the most careful investigation failed to reveal a trace of hostile occupation or passage. At the end of the bridge Jack got out of the car, leaving Tom Binns at the wheel, and ready to start at an instant's notice should there be a sudden attack.

"The tracks here don't show anything much," he said, looking up to Tom with a puzzled face. "I don't believe anything but a couple of farm wagons have passed this way to-day. If General Bliss thought this was his only line of advance, he'd have been certain to have had a few pickets here—or at least one of his scout cars. And I'll swear that nothing of that sort has happened here to-day. They'd have been bound to leave all sorts of traces, that's certain!"

"What do you think it means, Jack?"

"That there's something cooking and on the stove that we don't know about or suspect, even," said Jack. "I guess that General Bliss gets as good information as we do, and he must have figured out that he wouldn't be able to get here in time. If he went this way, anyhow, he'd have to leave Hardport in our possession behind him. And somehow I don't believe he'd do that."

"Say, Jack," called Tom Binns, suddenly, "I just saw a flash over there behind you—upon that hillock."

Jack began whistling indifferently. He strolled around, as if he were interested only in the view. Gradually he worked over closer to Tom and the big car, and then, and only then, he turned so that he could follow Tom's eyes with his own.

"I don't want anyone that's around here to think I'm looking at them," he said in a low tone to Tom. "What does it seem like to you, Tom? Scouts?"

"I think so, Jack. I caught just a glimpse, after I called to you, of something that looked like a Scout uniform. I think that they're watching us."

"That's much better," said Jack, greatly relieved. "It didn't seem natural, somehow, to find this place so deserted. Say, Tom, you can run the car, can't you?"

"Yes, if I don't have to go too fast."

"All right. I'm going to climb in. Then pull the hood pretty well over and run her slowly through the bridge. It's covered, you see, and they can't see us after we're on it. Then, as soon as we're under cover, I'm going to drop out. They can't see how many of us there are in the car. I'll stay behind, and you run on around the bend, drop out of the car, quietly, and leave it at the side of the road."

"Will that be safe, Jack? Couldn't anyone who came along run off with it?"

"Not if you take the spark plug out and put it in your pocket. That cripples the car absolutely, and you ought always to do that, even if you just leave a car outside a store for a couple of minutes when you go in to buy something. This car is great, too, because you don't have to crank it. It has a self-starting device, so that you can start the motor automatically without leaving your seat."

"All right, Jack. What am I to do after I leave the car?"

"Work up quietly into the woods there. When you get up a way, scout down easily, and try to trail them. You'll find traces of them up there on the ridge, I'm sure, if they're really up there. I'll do the same thing from the other side here. I think we've got a good chance to break one of their signalling relays, don't you see?"

"I'll take my flags along, shall I, Jack?"

"Good idea! No telling what we'll be able to find out and do here. All right— I'm going to drop out now!"

The car slowed down and he dropped off silently, and laughed as he saw Tom Binns guide the big machine off into the light beyond the covered bridge again. Then, the laughter gone from his face, he slipped cautiously back in the opposite direction, and at the entrance to the bridge dropped down to the bed of the creek. The season had been dry, and the water in the creek was very shallow. His plan was definite in his own mind, and he had had enough experience in scouting to know that there was at least a good chance of success in his enterprise, although a difficult one.

His destination was the ridge where Tom Binns had seen the flashing of red and white signal flags. Step by step now, climbing slowly and carefully, he made his way up the bank, sure that even if whoever was on the ridge had guessed the ruse of the way in which he had left the automobile, they would not be looking for an attack from the direction in which he was making his stealthy, Indian-like advance. Another reason for slow and deliberate progress was to give Tom Binns time to reach the ridge, and take up a position favorable for the playing of his part in the scheme.

Before him now, as he moved on, he could hear sounds of quiet and stealthy movement, and at last, standing before him, as he peeped through a small opening in the thick undergrowth, he could see a Boy Scout, standing stiff and straight, and working his signal flags. He had to stand on a high spot and in a clearing to do this, as otherwise, of course, his flags could not have been seen at any distance. Jack measured the place with his eyes. His whole plan would collapse if the body of the signalling Scout were visible from the next relay stations, but he quickly decided that only the flags would show.

From behind the Scout with the flags now came the call of a crow—caw, caw, caw!

Jack grinned as he answered it. For a moment a look of suspicious alertness showed on the face of the Blue Scout. He whirled around to face the sound behind him, and in the moment that his back was turned Jack sprang on him.

The Blue Scout put up a fine struggle, but he was helpless against the combined attack of Jack Danby and Tom Binns, who sprang to his comrade's aid as soon as he saw what Jack had done.

"Two to one isn't fair," gasped Jack as he sat on his prisoner's chest, "but we had to do it. This is war, you see, and they say all's fair in love and war. Who are you?"

"Canfield, Tiger Patrol, Twenty-first Troop, Hampton's Scouts," said the prisoner. "Detailed for Scout service with the Blue army. You got me fair and square. We caught one of your fellows near Mardean, we heard, soon after the war began. Sorry—but it's all in the game."

"How on earth did you get to me so quietly? I was watching you in the road by the bridge, and I thought you'd gone off in your car. You certainly fooled me to the queen's taste."

"Fortune of war," said Jack. "The car gave us a big advantage. You're not to blame a bit. I guess you'll be exchanged pretty soon, too. We'll give you for Warner, you see. He's the one of our Troop who was caught. And a fair exchange isn't any robbery."

"Have we got to tie him up?" asked Tom Binns.

"Not if he'll give his parole not to escape or accept a rescue," said Jack. "How about that, Canfield? Will you give me your word of honor? I'm Jack Danby, Assistant Patrol Leader of the Crow Patrol of Durland's Troop, and ranking as a corporal for the maneuvers in the Red army."

"I'll give you my parole all right," said Canfield. He saluted stiffly. "Glad to meet you, Corporal Danby. Sorry the tables aren't turned, though. We've got a special dinner for our prisoners to-night—but we haven't caught many prisoners yet, worse luck!"

"All right! See if the flags are just the same, Tom."

Tom Binns compared the flags captured from Canfield with those he himself carried.

"They're exactly the same," he said. "We can use either his or ours. It doesn't make any difference."

"That's good. Stand up there now, Tom, and see what's coming. Can you see the next stations on both sides?"

"Sure I can, Jack. They're wig-wagging like the very dickens now, asking Canfield here why he doesn't answer."

"Signal that he was watching a grey scout car of the Red army, going north," said Jack, with a laugh.

Canfield heard the laugh with a rueful smile.

"You're certainly going to mess things up!" he said. "I ought to be court-martialled for letting you break up our signal chain this way."

Meanwhile Tom Binns was working his flags frantically.

"O. K.," he reported to Jack. "Message coming!"

Jack sprang to his side, and together the two Red Scouts watched the flags flashing in the distance. Jack showed a good deal of excitement.

"Gee," he said, "this is all to the good! That's a message from General Bliss himself, I'll bet! See, Tom? He's sending orders to General Brown, who commands his right wing. They're going to swing around back toward Hardport in a big half-circle, of which this place where we are now is pretty nearly the centre. And it's the Newville road that's the line of their march, and not this road over the creek at all. That's nerve for you, if you like, because the Newville pike is right in our lines, and if we move fast we can turn that right wing right in on their center."

For half an hour they stayed there, realizing more and more with every passing minute that the whole Blue army was developing a great and sweeping attack on Hardport, and in a direction entirely different from that being taken by General Bean. The information so far obtained by General Harkness obviously was entirely misleading, and in sending General Bean to Cripple Creek, as he had, he had simply deprived himself of a brigade, and, as he would learn in the morning, when the attack would most certainly begin, weakened a vital part of his lines. Bean was moving directly away from the spot where the attack would be concentrated, and the enemy would be able, unless something were quickly done, to strike at the unprotected center of the Red line, drive right through it, and throw the main portion of his army, like a great wedge, between the two sections of the Red forces.

Jack's face grew grave as message after message confirmed his fears. He looked at his watch.

"We've got to get word of this to General Harkness," he said. "Tom, I'm afraid you'll have to stay here and take chances on being caught. I've got to get back to headquarters and tell General Harkness what we've learned here. And if we both go, and leave the relay broken here, they'll smell a rat at once, and investigate. There's enough of a trail here to show a blind man, much less a bunch of Scouts who are just as good in their State as we're supposed to be in our own, just what's happened. So you stay here, and I'll take Canfield along with me in the car and make my way back to headquarters. You'll be able to leave pretty soon, anyhow, because it will be too dark for effective long-range signalling less than an hour from now. You can do it all right, can't you?"

"Yes," said Tom Binns, pluckily. It was plain that he didn't like the prospect of staying there alone, but he could see the necessity as easily as Jack himself, and that there was no other way of meeting the circumstance that had arisen.

"Do your best, of course, to avoid being captured," said Jack, as he turned to go, with Canfield at his side. "But it will be no reflection on you if you are made a prisoner, and we won't need to feel that they've put one over on us if they catch you. We've got more than a fair return for the loss of even a First Class Scout in the information that they've unknowingly given us. It may mean the difference between the success and failure of the whole campaign."

"You're a wonder, Danby," said Canfield, as they made their way down to the car. Being on parole, of course, and, as a Boy Scout should always be, honorable and incapable of breaking his given word, Canfield made no attempt to escape or hamper Jack in any way. "I've heard a lot about you, and I'm glad to see you at work, even if it does make it bad for me. You seem to be able to tell just about what's going on around here. I couldn't do that. I didn't think about the larger meaning of the orders I was passing on."

"I may be wrong, you know," said Jack, as he waited for Canfield to step into the car before climbing into the driver's seat. "I'm really only making a guess, but I think it's a pretty good one. And, anyhow, with the notes I've got for him, General Harkness ought to be able to get a pretty good line on what's doing."

"He ought to be," admitted Canfield, regretfully, but smiling at the same time. "You're certainly one jim-dandy as a Scout! I'd hate to be against you in a real war. If you can handle things always the way you've done this time, you'd be a pretty hard proposition in a real honest-to-goodness fight."

CHAPTER VII

A TIMELY WARNING

Jack debated the advisability of meeting General Bean and telling him what he had learned, but he decided that since that detour would take up nearly half an hour of time that was now most valuable, he had better hurry right through to headquarters, and carry his news direct to the commander-in-chief. He cared little now for the danger of meeting stray detachments of the enemy. He was not afraid of them, since he knew that they would not, in all probability, be keeping a particularly careful watch for him, and he was confident of the ability of his car to outdistance any pursuit that might be attempted.

Twice, indeed, as he raced for Hardport, he met patrols of the enemy's cavalry, but he was burning up the ground at such a rate that they probably were not able to distinguish the nature of his car, especially as it was nearly dark.

"Gee, Danby, you certainly make this old car go!" said Canfield, admiringly. "She's a daisy, too. I never was in a car before that rode as easily as this, and I think you're going twice as fast as I've ever ridden in my life before."

Going at such speed, it did not take long for Jack to reach headquarters. He rushed at once into the hotel, and his earnest, dust-streaked face so impressed the officer on duty outside the General's door that he took Jack in at once.

"I have the honor to report that I have carried out your instructions, General," said Jack. "I have used more than the two hours you allowed me, but I felt that that was necessary."

Then he explained the capture he and Tom Binns had effected, and how, by taking the place of their prisoner with the flags, they had been able to discover the enemy's real plans.

General Harkness wasted no words then for a few minutes. He pressed two or three buttons, and, as staff officers answered, his orders flew like hail.

"Telegraph General Bean to change his route at once," he ordered, "and make Newville his objective point, throwing out heavy skirmish lines and advance pickets to prevent a surprise. He will march all night, if necessary— but he must be at Newville before five o'clock."

The officer who took the order saluted, turned on his heel, and left the room.

"Direct Colonel Abbey to bring up his cavalry regiment at once from Bremerton," was the next order. "He will march across the line, and then follow it until he reaches the Newville pike. Thence he will turn to support any movement General Bean may find it necessary to make there. Colonel

Abbey will not engage the enemy, however, even to the extent of feeling him out, without direct orders from either General Bean or myself. Repeat a copy of Colonel Abbey's orders to General Bean."

"That's good work, Danby, once more," he said, then, turning to Jack. "We'd have been in a nice mess if you hadn't discovered that. They masked their turning movement beautifully. If they had got hold of Newville and cut General Bean off from the main body of this army we would have had to abandon Hardport at once. General Bean would certainly have been captured, and we would have had to fall back on the capital, with an excellent prospect of being attacked and forced to fight at a great disadvantage on our retreat. As it is, even if General Bean is forced to circle around Newville, we can concentrate at Bremerton and fight on ground of our own choosing, though that would make this place untenable."

Receiving no further orders, Jack remained to listen. He stood at attention, and he enjoyed the experience of being in the room of a general on active service, for the constant stream of orders General Harkness was giving was hardly checked at all by his pause to speak to Jack and thank him for the good work he had done.

"Instruct Colonel Henry to complete preparations for the theoretical destruction of the railroad station, the sidings, and all passenger and freight cars now here," he directed next. "If we are forced to abandon the place, we will leave plenty of evidence behind us that it is no longer of any use to the enemy. Rather a dog-in-the-manger policy, I suppose—" this to Jack, since the officer had gone to obey the order—"but that's war. If you can't make any use of a town or a lot of supplies yourself, remember always that that is no reason why the enemy should not find them of the utmost service, and see to it that he can get no benefit from them. That was General Sherman's way. He left a trail of desolation fifty miles wide wherever he marched with his army, and he was always sure that the enemy, even if he came along after him, would find no chance to live in that country."

Jack offered no comment at all. He knew his place, as a Boy Scout, and, while he realized that it was a great compliment for the General to talk to him in that fashion, he had no intention of presuming on the fact.

Just then an orderly entered.

"Scout Thomas Binns, of Durland's Troop, General," he said, saluting. "He says he has important information."

"Another of you?" asked the General, smiling as he faced Jack. "Send him in!"

"He was with me in the car, sir," said Jack. "I left him behind when I came to make my report."

"I have the honor to report, General," said little Tom Binns, standing at the salute when he appeared, "that the enemy now has reason to believe that General Bean is advancing for Cripple Creek and will camp there to-night."

"How do you know that, my boy?" said the General.

"The signal station next to me on the side nearest Hardport flashed the news that General Bean had changed his course, sir," replied Tom. "I didn't think they ought to hear that at General Bliss's headquarters, so I changed the message in relaying it, and said that it was now positively determined that General Bean was heading for Cripple Creek, and would proceed to occupy the bridge. In fact, I added that his pickets were already in sight."

"Excellent!" laughed the General. "But how did you get here, my boy? I don't see how you escaped falling into their hands."

"That was the last message we got before dark, sir," said Tom. "After that we all got orders to report at their Scout headquarters, and I decided to try to make my way back here. On the way I ran into one of their outposts, and a man with a motorcycle chased me. But he had a puncture—I think that was because I dropped my knife in the road—and he had to stop to repair that. While he was doing it, I worked up behind him, and I managed to get the motorcycle and came on. I knew he'd have a good chance to catch me, because I didn't know the roads very well."

"Ha, ha!" laughed General Harkness. The incident seemed to amuse him immensely, for he laughed till the tears rolled down his cheeks. "I wish I had a whole army of you, my boy. We'd have little trouble with the enemy, then. Now you two can go back to Bremerton. That is likely to be nearer the scene of battle in the morning than this town, and you have both done a good day's work in any case. I am highly pleased with you. Carry my compliments to Captain Durland, and say to him that I shall be glad to see him in my headquarters in the morning. He will have to find out where they are, for I don't know myself at this moment. I shall probably be up most of the night myself, but do you be off now, and get a good night's rest. You have earned it."

So once more Jack drove the grey car to Bremerton. He was almost reeling with fatigue by this time, for it was nearly nine o'clock, and he had done enough since noon to tire out a full-grown man.

"That was mighty clever work of yours with the motorcycle," he said to Tom. "How did you ever think of it?"

"I didn't want to be caught, Jack, that's all. I guess you were right the other day when you said we never knew what we could do until we had to do it. It's certainly true with me, because if anyone had ever told me that I would do a thing like that, I'd have told them they were crazy."

"Well, whatever the reason was, it was good work. If they'd caught you with your signal flags, they might have smelled a rat, and the best part of our catching Canfield was that they didn't know anything about it. That's what made him such a very valuable prisoner for us to have."

CHAPTER VIII

THE ENEMY'S TRICK

Jack Danby was pretty tired after his exertions. Captain Durland, glad that his Troop, except for the one prisoner, poor Harry Warner, of the Raccoons, was still all together under his command in Bremerton, found quarters for them in the little village hotel.

"We'll turn in early," he said, "and get all the sleep we can. I think there'll be some hard fighting to-morrow, and we can't tell yet what part we'll be called on to play in it when it comes. So we'll get all the sleep we can. I shouldn't wonder if the battle to-morrow began long before dawn. If we can turn the right wing of the Blue army, which doesn't seem very likely now, we will want to start the action as soon as possible, because, when you have the enemy trapped, the thing to do is to strike at him just as quickly as you can. Every minute of delay you give him gives him just that much more of a chance to get out of the trap."

"That means if General Bean gets to Newville in time, doesn't it, sir?" asked Dick Crawford.

All the Scouts had listened with the greatest interest to what Jack had told them of his day's adventures. He had been at the very heart of things, and he was able, from the information that he and Tom Binns had intercepted, to get a complete view of the whole scene of the operations, far superior to that of any of the others, who knew, of course, only what was going on in their own immediate neighborhood.

"Yes—that's what I mean, of course," said Durland. "But it's a forlorn hope. There's a limit to human endurance. Even regular troops would call what Bean's brigade did before sunset a hard day's work. Just think of it—they were in motion before daybreak this morning, ready for their dash across the line. Then they marched several miles toward Hardport, turned aside for a big flanking movement, and had hardly occupied the city when they were started off for the Cripple Creek Bridge. Then they were turned off again from that, and sent to march another twenty miles to Newville. That was necessary, of course—they'd have been cut off and captured, to a man, if they'd kept on for the bridge, without even the fun of putting up a fight for their colors. But that doesn't make it any easier work. I know Bean—he won't ask his men to do the impossible. And that means that he'll be five miles from Newville when morning comes."

"Then nothing is likely to be decided to-morrow?" said Bob Hart.

"I don't see how it can be. The two armies are playing at cross purposes to-night, you see. Unless the Blues have corrected their mistake, they will be working on the assumption that Bean's brigade is out of it entirely, and that they can eat up the main body of our army, and then turn around and capture Bean when they like. While they're working on that idea, General Harkness is making a desperate effort to turn the tables on them, and lead them into just the same sort of a trap that Jack Danby has enabled him to escape. His strategy is perfectly sound, and he can't lose seriously, even if his plan fails. But I think the umpires will call the fight to-morrow a drawn battle."

"What will happen then?"

"Now you're asking a question I can't answer. We've got to wait more or less on the movements of the Blue army, you see. After all, we're on the defensive. Of course, we've taken the offensive to-day, and on the showing that's been made so far the Blues are very much out of it. On the single day the umpires would have to give the decision to General Harkness. He's in a better position right now to prevent an attack on the capital itself than he was before the war began."

Then Durland called the order to sound taps, and in a few minutes the Troop was sound asleep.

Bremerton that night was peaceful and quiet. Over in the telegraph office watchful soldier operators were at work, but the clicking of their keys did not disturb the Scouts in their well-earned rest. For miles all about them there was bustle and activity. Troops, exhausted after a day of work that was very real indeed for a good many of the militiamen, clerks and office workers, camped along the roads and took such rest as they could get. This game was proving as much of an imitation of war as many of them wanted to see.

They had come out expecting a restful, pleasant vacation, with the thrill of a war game as an additional incentive for them to turn out, but they were finding that it closely resembled hard work—the sort of work they got too little of in their crowded days of office routine. Later they would enjoy the recollection of it, but while they were doing it there was a good deal of roughing that wasn't so pleasant.

A late moon made the countryside brilliant, and easy to cover with the eye, and when, a couple of hours after midnight, the roll of rifle firing in the distance, coming like light thunder, awoke the Scouts, who were sleeping three in a room, many of them rushed to their windows.

Jack Danby shared a room with Pete Stubbs and Tom Binns, his particular chums, and he laughed at them.

"What are you looking for, powder smoke?" he asked them. "Don't you remember that they're using smokeless powder in this war? You couldn't see that firing if it were within a hundred yards."

The firing soon became general and Jack himself grew interested.

"That doesn't sound just like outposts coming together," he said. "It seems to me that it's pretty general firing, as if considerable bodies of men were getting engaged. I'd like to be out there and see what's going on."

The distant din increased, and there was no longer a chance for the Scouts to sleep. In real warfare tired men, it is said, can sleep with a battle raging all about them, but the Scouts weren't inured to such heavy firing yet, and it disturbed and excited them. Durland himself wasn't bothered, but he sensed the restlessness of his Troop, and he rose and dressed. One by one, too, the Scouts followed his example, and gathered on the big veranda of the village inn.

"Come on over to the telegraph office, Dick," said Durland. "Let's see if we can't find out who's kicking up all this fuss and what it's about."

The telegraph wires, which never slept, were clicking busily when the Scout-Master and his assistant entered the office.

"Abbey's cavalry running into the enemy on the Newville pike," said a tired operator, flicking a cigarette from his mouth as Durland spoke to him. "Funny, too! We thought he'd join General Bean before he saw a sign of the enemy."

Durland felt himself growing anxious; then laughed at himself for his own anxiety. He turned to find Dick Crawford at his elbow.

"I'm taking this thing too seriously, Dick," he said, with a smile. "After all, it's only a game. But I'd certainly like to know the inner meaning of that firing. Unless we've been grossly deceived, Abbey had no business to bump into any considerable force of the Blue army to-night."

"I guess we're all taking it pretty seriously, sir," said Dick. "Isn't that the right way, too? Of course, it's only a game—but we might be playing it seriously some time."

"You're right, Dick," said the Scout-Master. "We can't take this too seriously. I'm going to horn in here and see if there isn't something we can do."

He walked over to the key.

"See if you can report my Troop to General Harkness as ready for any service required," he said.

It took some little time for the operator to get the message through. Then, however, he sat back with a smile.

"I guess they'll be able to use you, all right, Captain," he said. "They seem to be a mile up in the air about what Colonel Abbey's doing. All the Colonel can report himself is that he's run into a considerable force, and he's engaging him tentatively. He seems to be afraid of being cut off if he goes on without feeling his way."

Then followed another delay.

"Here you are, Captain," said the operator, at last. "Coming, now!"

"Take it," said Durland. "I can read it as it comes."

Out of the chatter of the sounding key both Durland and Dick Crawford could make sense.

"Take your Troop up to Colonel Abbey," came the order. "Report to him for any service possible. But detail two Scouts, with automobile, to make an attempt to discover the nature of the enemy's operations on the Newville road beyond the point where Colonel Abbey's command has engaged the enemy. General Bean is within three miles of Newville, waiting for daylight, owing to the firing in that direction. It is most important to apprise him of the actual conditions."

"Report that orders are received and will be obeyed at once," Durland flung back to the operator, and he and Crawford hurried from the building to rejoin the Scouts, who were waiting eagerly on the porch of the hotel for any news that might come.

"Get ready to hike," ordered Dick Crawford, as he reached the Scouts. "Danby, report to Captain Durland at once."

Jack listened to his instructions carefully.

"This is a harder job than any you've had yet, Jack," said his commander. "But it counts for more, too. Are you sure you're not too tired to handle your car?"

"Not a bit of it, sir!" protested Jack. "I've had all the sleep I need. What the General wants to know chiefly is whether there are enough troops of the enemy between Colonel Abbey and Newville to prevent a junction between the cavalry and General Bean's brigade, isn't it?"

"Right! I can't give you any special orders. You'll have to use your own judgment, and do whatever seems best when the time comes. This is the sort of a situation that changes literally from minute to minute, and if I gave you special orders before you started they would probably hamper you more than they helped you."

"Can I have Tom Binns again, sir?"

"Certainly! I'll have Crawford tell him to report to you at the garage. Overhaul your car carefully—you don't want any little mechanical trouble to come along and spoil your work just as you are on the verge of success."

"The car's all right, sir. I went over every bit of it before I turned in. I had an idea I might be called for some sort of emergency work when every minute would count, and she's ready for any sort of a run right now."

"Good enough! That's the way to be. 'Be prepared'—that's a pretty good motto. It has certainly been proved abundantly in the last few hours."

It would take the Scouts a good three hours to come up with Colonel Abbey's regiment of cavalry, but Jack and Tom Binns, in the big grey car that moved silently, like a grey ghost, in the moonlight, were well ahead of them as the column swung out of the little town.

"Well, we're off again!" said Jack. "No telling what's going to come up before the night's over, either, Tom. We've got a roving commission, with no orders to hold us down, and I'm out to see just as much as the road will show us."

"Are you going to stick to the main road, Jack?"

"No. There's a cross road a little way beyond here. If they've blocked Colonel Abbey's advance on this road, we couldn't get beyond his position, anyhow, and it won't do us any good to get as far as that and no further. It's what they're doing beyond there that General Harkness wants to know."

"Where is the main body of our army now, Jack?"

"Right around Hardport. The only troops that are moving to-night are Abbey's cavalry regiment, and General Bean's brigade. General Bean, with the rest of the army closing toward him, is to hold the enemy in check if they occupy Newville before we get to the place ourselves. The rest of the army, at Hardport, can move to his support, or it can develop a big flanking movement that will bring Bremerton into the centre of our line, with the forces toward Newville making a sort of a triangular wedge stuck out in front. That wedge, you see, will have the whole army as a reserve. It isn't as favorable a situation as if they had made for Cripple Creek, for there we would have been in a position to force them back on Smithville, where they mobilized."

"They'd have gone right into a trap if they had kept on for Newville, wouldn't they?"

"Yes; but that was too much for us to hope for, really. It's good enough as it is. It was General Harkness's plan from the first to make a stand at Bremerton, unless they gave him the chance to make it an offensive campaign. The mistake we made in sending a brigade to Cripple Creek more than made up for the capture of Hardport, however, and so we lost that chance. If we could have made sure of Newville to-night, nothing could have saved the Blue army."

"Who's to blame for that, Jack?"

"No one. You can't expect the enemy to tell you what he's going to do, and even Napoleon couldn't always guess right. I think we'll beat them all right— that is, I don't think they'll get within twenty miles of the capital in the time they've got, even if we get badly beaten in this battle that's starting now."

"Here we are at the cross roads, Jack. Which way are you going now?"

"Toward Mardean, at first. I'm going to swing in a great big circle around Hardport, and way beyond it. I want to come down on them from behind and see just as much as I can."

"If you swing very far around that way it'll take you pretty near Smithville, won't it?"

"That's just where I want to get, Tom. The place to find out what the enemy is going to do is the place where he is doing it, it seems to me."

Hardport, a patch of light against the sky, held little interest for Jack. The road he took swung back toward the State line, so that he passed very near Hardport before he reached the road that he and Tom had first traveled when they crossed the line at full speed after war had been declared. But Mardean wasn't held by the enemy now. The troops that had crossed there had been recalled after the capture of Hardport and the wreck of the early Blue plans, and some of them probably were in Hardport now as prisoners of war, but with none of the rigors commonly attaching to imprisonment to distress them.

"This road is safer than it was when we took it before," said Jack. "Remember how we had to take to the fields a little way along here? That was pretty exciting."

"You bet it was, Jack! I'm glad we can stick to the roads here."

"Don't be too glad yet, Tom. No telling what we may have to do before the night's over, you know. It's early yet—or late, as you happen to look at it."

Mile after mile of road, looking like a silver streak in the moonlight, dropped beneath the wheels of the big grey car. They sped around and beyond Hardport, and Jack, studying his road map, lighted now by a little electric light, began to slow down, since they were in country where it was possible, though not probable, that the enemy's outposts might be encountered.

"I've got an idea that they're marching hard and fast to-night," said Jack. "Somehow, I'm not easy in my mind. I'm afraid they may have had some way of finding out what our army was doing. You know that we're not the only people who can detect concealed and covered movements. And they may be setting a trap for us again, just as they were doing when General Bean was drawn off toward Cripple Creek."

"I've lost track of where we're going, Jack. Where does this road we're on now come from?"

"Practically straight from Mardean. You see, Mardean will be about the right of our army to-morrow. A brigade will drop back that way from Hardport, if we give up that town in the morning, and the main force will move for Bremerton."

"Then if the enemy should happen to get around this way and break over the State line near Mardean, they'd be in a good position to meet us to-morrow, wouldn't they?"

"First rate! But that's not the idea, at all. They're all over in the other direction, nearer Bremerton, and east of Hardport. The trouble Colonel Abbey encountered seems to indicate that it's their plan to cross in force near Bremerton. That's why holding Newville would be so important to them."

Now Jack threw in the high speed again. And at once, almost, as the car sped on, something about the song of the throbbing engine bothered Jack. In a moment he had shifted his gears, and in another, the car, coughing and rattling, came to a sudden stop.

"Good thing I heard that," said Jack, a few moments later, "or we'd have been stuck properly a few miles further on. Won't take me five minutes to fix it now."

As he tinkered on the machine, his ears were busy, and he and Tom heard the sound of approaching horses in the same instant. At once Jack leaped to his driver's seat, and ran the car through an open fence into a field beside the road.

"I want to see what's doing here," he said. "That doesn't sound very good to me."

The trouble with his engine had been providential, for ten minutes later he realized that had he gone on at full speed he would have encountered the advance guard of at least a full division of the enemy.

Quietly and steadily the Blue troops were marching on. There was purpose in the look of them, and a grim earnestness that made Jack whistle.

"Tom," he whispered, "you certainly hit it! They're setting a trap all right. They're going to cross at Mardean and swing around to cut off our troops from Bremerton. They've got a nice plan—just to steal our position, and make us fight on our ground—but with positions reversed."

CHAPTER IX

JACK DANBY'S GOOD NEWS

Hardly daring to breathe lest they be heard, the two Scouts waited while the Blue troops passed. It took more than two hours for the regiments, marching in close order, to get by them, and it was nearly light when the last stragglers had passed their hiding-place.

"Gee," cried Jack, "that's certainly a surprise to me! Say, Tom, do you know what they've done? They've buffaloed General Bean, and fooled him completely—and our whole army! They've left not more than two regiments there. Of course, that was a stronger force than Abbey had, but they managed it so cleverly that they're holding up General Bean and his whole brigade."

"How can that be, Jack? I thought the umpires decided on the strength and the probable result of any encounter between the armies—and they surely couldn't decide that two regiments could beat a brigade?"

"No—but if the two regiments masked their real weakness so cleverly that they weren't attacked by the brigade, there wouldn't be anything for the umpires to decide—and that's what I'm afraid of. That's clever tactics, you see, and they'd get the credit for it, of course—and they'd deserve it, too. Well, here's where we stop loafing. We've got to cut a telegraph wire somewhere and get word of the true state of affairs to General Harkness. He can't wait until full daylight to move his troops now."

"What good will cutting a wire do, Jack?"

"Lots of good, Tom. This car has a regular apparatus for cutting in on a wire, and a set of sending and receiving instruments. If we cut the wire, it goes dead until we connect it with our instruments. Then only the section beyond where we cut in is dead. There's a telegraph wire direct from Hardport to Smithville. Cutting the wire is legitimate, even in the war game, because it's necessary to do the actual cutting. It isn't like the railroad, which can be destroyed theoretically, and left actually ready for use."

Jack had started his car, still running through the fields when the troops had passed, and now, looking carefully at the telegraph poles and wires, he dropped from his seat and, with wire cutters and repair tools, and his pocket set of instruments, he proceeded to put into practice the theory that he had explained to Tom. He cut the wire neatly and carefully. Then he connected the broken end with his instruments, completing the circuit again, and began calling for General Harkness's headquarters in Hardport.

"See how it's done, Tom?" he asked. "Easy when you know how, you see."

"Yes; it's like lots of other things that way, Jack. The trouble is you always seem to know just how to do things like that and I never do."

"Got 'em!" cried Jack, enthusiastically, at that moment, and began at once to send his important news.

"I want to get permission now to go on and tell General Bean what we've learned," he explained to Tom as he still waited after sending his message. "Then, as soon as I get it, I'll splice this wire and fix it so that the line will be open for regular service again. We don't want to interrupt traffic by telegraph or telephone, if we can help it. But this won't make much difference at this hour of the night. I don't believe that many messages are sent over this wire after midnight as a rule."

They had to wait twenty minutes for the reply, but when it came Jack was told to use his own best judgment, and that General Harkness would rely upon him to get the highly important information he had sent to headquarters to General Bean.

"I thought we'd be allowed to do that," said Jack, after he had put the wire in order again. In the car there was plenty of telegraph wire for repairing lines cut by the enemy, so the task was not at all a difficult one.

"Gee, Jack," said Tom, "I've certainly learned one thing lately, and that is that there's nothing you know that isn't likely to come in handy sometime or another. I didn't know you knew as much as this about telegraphy."

"I've always been interested in it, Tom. It's so fascinating. You can use all sorts of knowledge if you're in the army, too. Think of the engineers. They have to be able to build bridges, and destroy them, and erect fortifications without the proper materials. Not in this war, of course, but if there was real fighting. These maneuvers are different from the ordinary sort. They're not so cut and dried, and there aren't so many rules. I've read about maneuvers when there were rules to govern every sort of situation that came up—in fact, surprising situations couldn't come up, because everything that was to happen had been worked out ahead of time."

"This is better for us, isn't it, Jack? I mean, we're really learning how a war would actually be fought."

"We're getting a pretty good idea of it, anyhow. It isn't a bit the way I thought it was going to be."

"Well, we ought to be getting in touch with General Bean pretty soon, I should think."

"We've got another ten or twelve miles to drive yet. I took a pretty wide swing around, thinking we'd avoid the enemy altogether. Instead of that, we bumped right into them. It's surely a good thing we had that little engine trouble. We'd be prisoners right now if we'd been able to go on at full speed, because I don't believe we'd have been able to see them in time to turn around and get away. And we got a much better chance to see what they were up to, too."

As they approached General Bean's brigade the firing in the direction of Bremerton, where Colonel Abbey had encountered the enemy, began to be audible again. It had died away for a time, and Jack had wondered whether Abbey had retired. The sound of the heavy rifle fire, however, with an occasional explosion of a shell to make it louder, reassured him.

Newville was deserted when they entered it, and Jack laughed. Not a Blue soldier was in sight—and yet General Bean was waiting for full daylight, convinced that the main body of the Blue army was there.

"They certainly did make a clever shift," he said to Tom. "General Bliss has a reputation for moving quickly, and striking like a snake. He covers his movements well, and I'll bet that if we ever do have another war, he'll cut a pretty big figure. Captain Durland says he's a real fighter, of the sort that was developed in the Civil War. Some of the best fighters on both sides in that war, you know, were men who never went to West Point at all."

"The great generals were regulars, though, weren't they?"

"Most of them, yes. Grant, Sherman, Sheridan, Lee—they were all West Pointers, and a lot more of them, too. But there were others. They say, in the histories, that a great crisis brings up the men to meet it. It's perfectly true that Grant and Sherman had been in the regular army, but they had resigned before the war, and they hadn't made good particularly before that, either in the army or afterward, when they went into business. It was the war that made them famous, and a good many others, too."

They had turned now toward Hardport, and the pickets of General Bean's waiting brigade, eagerly looking for the enemy, were in sight. Time after time they were challenged and stopped, but Jack, despite questions from officers and men, all eager for the news they were sure he was bringing, since his exploits had already won him a considerable reputation in the Red army, refused to tell what he knew to anyone save General Bean himself. They did not have to go all the way to the rear of the army. General Bean himself, small, wiry, active and peppery, met them soon after they had come into the midst of his lines. He was riding his big, black horse, and, although he had had no sleep that night, he looked fresh and ready for another day in the saddle.

"Hum," he said, pulling his moustache, as he listened to them, "they fooled us, didn't they? Captain Jenks, you will give my compliments to Colonel Jones, and instruct him to put his regiment in motion at once. We will occupy Newville, and then close in on the enemy, supporting Colonel Abbey by an attack on the enemy's rear."

He rubbed his hands together delightedly as the officer rode off to give the order.

"Do you know the enemy's position now?" he asked Jack. "He's the nut, and Abbey and I are the crackers. You've done good work. This is the second time within twenty-four hours that the information you have obtained has rescued us from a situation of a good deal of danger. Did you learn what General Harkness's plans were?"

"He intends moving at once to Bremerton, sir," said Jack. "The enemy, as nearly as I could guess, was heading for that place, planning to cross the line by the Mardean road, and then swing cast to Bremerton."

"Right! That's what they must intend to do. Well, I reckon they will find we're ready for them, and that we'll hold a position that the umpires will have to give us credit for."

The brigade was already in motion while they spoke. The men had bivouacked in their lines, as they had marched, and the whole section of country was lighted with their fires. In the faint light of dawn, growing stronger every minute now, the twinkling fires had a strange and ghost-like effect.

"Looks like the real thing, doesn't it?" asked General Bean. "I wish I'd had such a chance when I was a boy as you have now. We don't ever want another war—but there's no use acting as if it was beyond the range of possibility, and the next best thing to not fighting at all is knowing how to do it and getting it over quickly when it does become inevitable. If I had my way these maneuvers would take place in a score of different parts of the country every year. It isn't asking much to ask the militia to turn out for one week of the fifty-two, and a week of this sort of thing is worth a year of ordinary drill and theory work in armories. I don't mean that the drill isn't useful; it is. But it isn't everything, as we've seemed inclined to think. This sort of work, and constant practice at the ranges is what makes soldiers. These fellows, if they ever go to a real war, won't have to work any harder than my brigade has had to work in the last few hours. They're so tired now that they haven't got enough energy to know they are tired. They'd just as soon march as rest—and that's the way they ought to be. Do 'em good!"

Jack led the way of Colonel Jones's regiment into Newville, and then turned down the pike. The firing in front was very sharp now. And soon it was redoubled, as the advance of the main body of General Bean's brigade came into touch with the Blue troops who had so decidedly worried Abbey during the night.

Finally, on the crest of a hill which overlooked the valley beneath, Jack stopped the car.

"This is a splendid chance to see a battle on a small scale, Tom," he said. "There's nothing else for us to do now—we might as well take a look at things."

There was light enough now to make it worth while to stop and look on. Abbey's men were dismounted. In a field a mile or so back of the line of battle they could see the horses of his regiment, hobbled, and under guard. Before them, lower down, was the enemy, doing little of the firing, and with his real strength pretty well masked. And, as they knew, Bean's troops were advancing slowly, ready to take them in the rear, and cut them off.

"Where are the umpires?" asked Tom.

"They're somewhere around—trust them for that!" said Jack. "They're not only supposed to umpire, but they've got to make a detailed report of all the operations to the War Department, and criticize everything that both armies do, too. The firing brought them up as soon as it began, you may be sure."

Slowly but steadily and surely the drama unfolded itself before their fascinated eyes. They could see the slow advance of Abbey's dismounted troopers as soon as the firing in the enemy's rear convinced them that the support they had been awaiting had come at last. And before long the enemy was completely surrounded by a chain of Red troops, firing steadily. It lasted for nearly twenty minutes and then a bugle blew, over to their right, and in another moment the "Cease Firing" call had passed from regiment to regiment. The appeal to the umpires had been made, and now the troops that had been seeking all possible cover showed themselves, that the umpires might inspect the position and see whether there was any possible chance for the entrapped regiments of the Blue army to extricate themselves.

"They hung on too long," said Jack. "They ought to have begun their retreat before daylight. Then they might have been able to fall back and slip away and around to join the main Blue army at Mardean. I'm afraid they'll all be written down as captured now."

Jack was right in his idea, too. The umpires, after a careful inspection of the situation, decided that General Bean's tactics had been successful.

"You are to be congratulated, General," said a Brigadier General of the regular army, the chief umpire, riding up to the militia commander. "A very neat evolution, carefully planned and worked out. We were inclined to think that they had fooled you. Abbey was in a bad way until you came up. But you came out very well."

CHAPTER X

THE SCOUTS MEET AN OLD FRIEND

Jack Danby's clever scouting had changed the entire situation. The capture of his two regiments made General Bliss's situation decidedly precarious. His case was not hopeless yet, by any means, since, as the attacking force, the Blue army had been the stronger to begin with, because the War Department had so arranged matters that the advantage of position favored the Red forces sufficiently to make up for the superior force of General Bliss. General Bean's quick following up of the information Jack had given, however, had enabled the Red army to equalize the forces of the contending armies, and General Harkness, who threw a cavalry brigade into Bremerton within three hours of the timely warning Jack sent him, was now in no danger of being forced to fight on ground where his original advantage of position would be transferred to the enemy.

Now the position was one of open tactics. The lines were drawn, and some sort of a battle would have to be fought, theoretically, before further movements were in order. With Bremerton as his centre, General Harkness and his army lay directly across the line of the Blue advance, already across the border at Mardean, and seeking, or intending, rather, to seek the control of the railroad at Fessenden Junction, a dozen miles back of Bremerton.

The Junction was the key to the situation now, so far as the hopes of the invading forces were concerned. Its possession would, theoretically, cut the defenders off from their base of supplies, and, once it was captured, General Bliss would force the Red army immediately to fall back and occupy the defenses of the capital city itself, since the railroad would enable him to cut off its supplies and advance his troops against it with great speed. That would mean the immediate abandonment of any offensive tactics on the part of General Harkness, and would make up for the capture of the two regiments that General Bean had sent into Bremerton as prisoners of war.

But there seemed little chance of an engagement on Tuesday. Ever since noon the day before, when hostilities had begun, both armies had been constantly on the march. There had been severe fighting, and the plans of the commanders had involved the rapid movement of considerable bodies of troops. As a result, the troops on both sides were nearly exhausted. In the first place, they did not have the stamina that is the portion of regular troops. They were, in the main, militiamen, clerks, lawyers, brokers, and men of that sort, who do not have the chance of regular exercise, and who do not keep such strict hours as do trained soldiers.

"There'll be no fighting until to-morrow, in my opinion," said Durland, when Jack and Tom reported to him; "it's a pretty situation as it stands now, but these fellows can't do any more. Bean's brigade in particular must be about ready to drop. I never saw troops worked harder. They've done mighty well, and, while there won't be any formal arrangement to that effect, I suppose, I guess that both generals will understand that they can't accomplish any more without some rest. They'd have to recognize that in a war, for the wise general never requires his men to fight when exhausted, except in the case of attack."

The Scouts retained their headquarters in Bremerton, which was now, after the abandonment of Hardport, headquarters for the Red army, also. But General Harkness had his headquarters in tents, despising the chance to use the small hotel of the town. He was exceedingly busy with his plans. General Bean had come in from the lines facing the enemy, who had been forced, reluctantly enough, to shift their base of attack, so that Newville was the focus of their semi-circular advance. Other brigade commanders and other high officers with them had also come in, and for the first time since hostilities had begun, General Harkness was able to consult with his subordinate officers.

"I guess the strategy of the campaign for the next two days will be pretty well worked out about now," said Durland, glancing over toward the tent of General Harkness, from which the smoke of the cigars and pipes of the officers was curling.

Before General Harkness's tent two orderlies were waiting. Now, suddenly, one of them, evidently hearing a call inside, answered it, and a few seconds later went off. He returned presently with a young officer of militia, and a few minutes later that officer came over to the Scout headquarters.

"Captain Durland?" he began, then broke off. "Great Scott!" he cried, "it's my old friend the Scout-Master, isn't it? I had no idea it was your Troop that was doing so well here."

"Jim Burroughs! Is that really you? I'm glad to see you!" exclaimed Durland.

Jack Danby, Tom Binns, Pete Stubbs and the rest of the Scouts, with happy memories of their days at Eagle Lake, and of the time when they had turned out in the woods at night to search for Burroughs and Bess Benton, crowded around to greet the young militia officer.

"I'm a lieutenant in the Sixteenth Regiment," said Burroughs. "Captain Durland, you're wanted in the General's tent. I went there to make a report, and he asked me to tell you to come to him at once."

Then the Scouts and Burroughs, who had nothing else to do for the time, began to exchange reminiscences and talk over old times.

"I've been hearing a lot about the good work a Scout called Danby was doing in one of the new scouting autos," said Jim Burroughs, "but somehow I didn't have any idea that it was a Boy Scout they were talking of. But I might have guessed it! If it hadn't been for you when we had the forest fires up at the lake, Camp Benton would have been wiped out."

"Oh, I guess you'd have managed all right with the guides," said Jack. "You always try to make out that I do more than I do, Jim. You must be trying to give me a swelled head."

"No danger of that, I guess," said Burroughs, laughing. "You're pretty level-headed, young man. By the way, I heard you had some trouble lately with a man called Broom. Anything in that?"

Jack's face darkened. Jim was bringing up a painful subject. But Pete Stubbs spoke up for him.

"Trouble?" he said. "Well, I guess yes, Mr. Burroughs! You heard about how Jack broke up the plot to wreck the train and rob it when he and Tom Binns were on a hike together?"

Jim nodded.

"Well, Broom was mixed up with that gang in some fashion. Then, afterward, we found that he was really after Jack. You know all about Jack's queer life up at Woodleigh—about Old Dan and all that?"

"I know that Jack never knew much about himself—his real name and who his mother and father were. You're still trying to find out about all that, aren't you, Jack?"

"You bet I am!" said Jack, his face lighting up at the thought. "And I'm going to do it, too!"

"Well, this Broom," Pete Stubbs went on, "was trying to find out where Jack had gone from Woodleigh. He didn't know that our Jack was the one he was looking for, or we don't know what he'd have done. So he had a double reason to be after him, though all he knew was that Jack might give dangerous evidence against those pals of his who were mixed up with the train business."

"I see! He was really playing against himself, without knowing it, wasn't he?"

"Yes. That was the funny part of it. Well, Broom and some other crooked people got an old gentleman and his daughter to trust them. The old gentleman, whose name was Burton, was looking for a boy, his brother's son, who was kidnaped when he was a baby. We think it may be Jack, and we're going to try to find out. Broom made the Burtons think that he could find the boy they were looking for, and he got a lot of money out of them."

"Gee, Pete, that sounds pretty interesting! Was that how the trouble came with Broom?"

"One of the ways, yes. When we were down at the shore a little while ago they tried to get hold of Jack. One night there was a pretty bad storm, and that was the night they picked out. Jack and I, with Mr. Durland and Dick Crawford, went out to rescue the Burtons, who had been left on their yacht, and when we got back some of us caught Broom and a friend of his. But they were rescued afterward by the sailors who had quit the yacht, and Jack raced into Wellbourne, and got most of them arrested. But Broom got away, in some fashion, after they had taken him to jail. So we don't know what's become of him."

"How about the Burtons, Pete? Have you found out yet whether they're really Jack's long-lost relatives or not?"

"No, not yet. Mr. Burton was terribly ill after the wreck of his yacht. He was exposed to the sea and the wind for a long time that night, you see, and as soon as he could be moved, he was sent to Europe by his doctor. Until they get back we sha'n't be able to tell for certain."

"I'm glad they're over there, anyhow," said Jack, breaking in. "I think they're safe from Broom over there."

"I'll tell you someone that isn't glad, though," said red-headed Pete Stubbs, mischievously. "That's Dick Crawford!"

The Assistant Scout-Master, who hadn't heard the conversation that had preceded Pete's mischievous remark, came up just then.

"What is it that doesn't make me glad like everyone else?" asked Dick, unsuspiciously, and everyone laughed.

"Discovered, Dick!" cried Jim Burroughs, laughing. "I hear that a certain beautiful young lady has charmed you—the one man I knew that I thought was proof against the ladies!"

Dick flushed furiously, but he saw that there was no use in attempting to deny the charge. He seized Pete Stubbs, jestingly, by the neck, however, and shook him hard.

"I've a good mind to give you the licking of your young life, you red-headed rascal!" he cried, but there was no malice in his tone, and Pete knew that the threat would never be carried out.

"I didn't do anything but tell the truth," protested Pete. "Let go of me, Dick! If it wasn't true, you wouldn't be so mad!"

"He's right, Dick, my boy," said Burroughs, much amused. "We've caught you with the goods. It's nothing to be ashamed of—we all do it, sooner or later, you know. You've done well to escape the charms of the other sex so long, it seems to me."

Then the Scouts began to drift away, and Dick and Jim Burroughs were left alone.

"Did they tell you of the way Jack's been pursued by this fellow Broom?" asked Dick.

"They told me enough to worry me, Dick. We mustn't let anything happen to that boy."

"I'd a good deal rather have something happen to me, Jim. But he's shown that he's pretty well able to take care of himself. Down at the beach there we all helped, but he was the one who really beat them, after all, when it came to the point. They were mighty determined. I think myself that they know who he is, although Jack himself and some of the others don't. But my idea is that there is a very queer secret about him, that they know all about it, and that they think it is to their advantage to keep Jack from learning the truth and also to keep those who may be looking for him from finding him."

"How about these Burtons, Dick? Do you really think that Jack is the boy they're looking for, or is that just one of Pete's wild guesses?"

"Miss Burton and I have talked that over two or three times, and while we're not sure, owing to Mr. Burton's illness, which made it impossible for us to discover certain things which would probably have made matters clear, we both agree that it looks very much as if Jack were the one. She thinks so, anyway, and she's quite prepared to acknowledge him as her cousin."

"Is she pretty, Dick, you sly old fox?"

"She certainly is, Jim! You can't tease me about her. I'm crazy about her, and I don't care who knows it. But she'd never look at me, I know that!"

"You can't tell, Dick. They're funny that way. You'd never think that Bess Benton would have any use for me, but we're engaged, and we're going to be married in a few months. Never give up hope, old chap! You've got as good a chance as anyone else. What more do you want?"

"Well, I'm not going to worry about that now, anyhow, Jim. She'll be away for some time yet, I'm afraid. And I've got to wait until I'm doing better than I am now before I can even think about getting engaged, much less married."

"You can think about it as much as you like, Dick, and it will do you good. The more you think about it, the harder you'll work and the better you'll get on. I've found that out, and I guess it's true with most of us."

"I guess the council's over, Jim. Here comes Captain Durland, and the other officers seem to be leaving, too. I wonder what's doing."

"Nothing much, probably. But I'll leave you to find out and get back to my regiment."

CHAPTER XI

AN INTENTIONAL BLUNDER

"You're wanted for duty again, Jack," said Captain Durland, when he returned from the council of war in General Harkness's tent.

"I'm all ready, sir," said Jack. "Gee, I think I've had it easy, riding around in an automobile, when all the rest of the fellows were scouting on foot."

"You'll make up for it, if you have been having it any easier," said the Scout-Master, with a smile. "This job that you've got on your hands now means a whole lot of work. You're to go to Fessenden Junction first, and make a detail map of the tracks about the depot there. I don't know just why it's wanted, or why it wasn't done before, but that's none of our business. Then when that's done, you're to bring it back here. After that I guess you'll have plenty more to do. But I won't tell you about the rest of it until you've finished that."

"Am I to go alone?" asked Jack.

"No. I want it done as quickly as possible, so you'd better take Peter Stubbs and Tom Binns along with you. Divide the work up and it won't take you very long. That's the easy part of it."

The Boy Scouts had studied map-making from a practical, working point of view, and it was no sort of a job for the three of them to make the required map.

"I see why they need this map, all right," said Jack. "There are a whole lot of new tracks in here, and the whole yard has been changed around within the last few weeks. That explains it. The old maps wouldn't be of much use for anyone who was depending on them for quick understanding of the railroad situation here."

"Now," said Durland, when they returned, "I've got the most difficult task that's been assigned to you yet, Jack. You've got only about one chance in a thousand of succeeding in it, but it's my own plan, and I'll be very pleased and proud if you do accomplish it. I want two of you to take the car, get inside the enemy's lines, with or without the car, as far as you can, and then get yourselves taken prisoners. What we want is for you to be near enough to General Bliss's headquarters to get some sort of an inkling of the nature of the attack that will be made.

"There is a dangerous weakness of the position here, which could hardly have been foreseen when the campaign was laid out in advance. That is, anyone getting control of Tryon Creek, which is practically dry in the summer, is in a position to dominate one side of the prospective battlefield. There are two lines of attack open to General Bliss. If he chooses Tryon

Creek we must keep him from occupying it at all costs. To do that we would have to uncover the other side—the road from Mardean."

"I'm to try to find out which line of attack they will follow, then, sir? Is that it?" asked Jack.

"Yes. We must know before the actual attack begins, or it will be too late. Now I want you to understand my plan. I haven't thought of the details, because they will depend absolutely on conditions as you may find them to be. But here is the outline. Three of you will take the car. You, Jack, and one other Scout will leave that, when there is no longer a chance of continuing to use it, and proceed on foot until you are well within the enemy's lines. Then you will manage to get captured, while seeming to make an effort to escape."

"Are we to give our parole then, sir?"

"On no account! But pretend to be frightened and discouraged. That is legitimate. You mustn't give your word not to attempt to escape, because that is an essential part of the plan. I have an idea that they will not keep a very close watch on you, and that you will find it quite possible to make a dash for liberty after dark. But before you do that you must try to discover where the attack is to be made, by keeping your ears open and your eyes as well, for possible movements of guns. Then you can try to get away, rejoin the automobile, and get back to our lines. Do you understand?"

"Yes, sir, I do! I think Pete Stubbs would be a good one to go with me, with Tom Binns to look after the car, because he knows how to drive it. Then if Pete and I couldn't both get away, one of us ought to be able to manage it, I should think, anyhow."

"That's the reason for sending two of you, of course," said Durland. "It's an outside chance, but you've done things almost as difficult. Remember that you must exercise the utmost caution. In time of real warfare no enterprise could be more dangerous, and the mere fact that there is no actual danger involved now is no reason for you to grow careless, though I need hardly give you such a warning."

"I'll do my best, sir," said Jack, enthusiastically. "It would certainly be a great joke on them if we could work it."

"Well, do the best you can. I don't want you to think that I really expect you to succeed. I think the chances are desperate. But, even if you cannot escape, there will be no difficulty about exchanging you, for we have a great many of their prisoners, including a number of officers, and they will be very glad to get them back. Otherwise I am sure General Harkness would never have consented to let you make the effort."

"If this were real war, and they saw us trying to escape, they would fire at us, wouldn't they?" asked Jack. "What I want to know is whether we're assumed to be shot, and have to stop if they see us and get a shot?"

"Yes, at any range less than a hundred yards. Above that range a prisoner escaping is supposed to have a good chance to get away. He has to stop, but need not show himself, and unless he is found he can resume his attempts to escape."

Then Durland explained briefly to Pete Stubbs and Tom Binns the parts they were assigned to play in this newest development of the war game, and, thrilling with excitement, they took their seats with Jack in the grey scout car.

"It won't be dark for a couple of hours yet," said Jack. "I think that's a good thing because we couldn't get very far in the enemy's lines with this car in daylight. So I'm going to take a long circle again and come down on them from behind. I'm not sure of where General Bliss's quarters are, but I should think they were probably pretty near Newville. If we come down the Newville pike from the direction of Smithville, it will be safe enough. Their watch will be closer in this direction, and by going around for about fifty miles we can manage that easily enough."

"Gee, you talk about driving a car fifty miles the way I would about getting on the trolley car at home," said Pete, admiringly.

"If you can drive at all, it isn't much harder, if you've got the time, to drive fifty miles than it is to drive five," said Jack. "And this time it's a lot safer. It's certainly one time when the longest way around is the shortest cut. We don't want to be caught until about ten o'clock, Pete. You understand that."

They roared through Smithville as it began to get dark, and then down the Newville pike. Jack slowed down when he was sure that he had plenty of margin in time, and through the growing dusk they saw the campfires of the Blue army springing up in all directions before them.

"Gee, there must be an awful lot of them," said Pete. "This is the closest I've been to them since we got started. You know, it makes me feel kind of shivery, even though I know that they won't do anything to us when they do catch us, Jack."

"That just shows that you really get into the spirit of it," said Jack, laughing happily. "If we remembered all the time that this was only a game, we wouldn't be doing things the right way at all. If you feel a little scary, and something like the way you'd feel if it was a real enemy in front of us, it'll only make you a bit more careful, and that's just what we want. We want them to think, when they catch us, that we're surprised and scared, and if we can make ourselves feel that way, so much the better. It's much easier to make other people believe a thing if you half believe it yourself, even if you know down at the bottom of your heart it isn't so at all."

A few rods farther on Jack swerved the car into a field.

"Here's a good place to stop, I guess," said Jack. "It's pretty quiet here, and we'll get along, Pete, and find out as much as we can before we let them catch us. You'll be all right here, Tom. Turn the car around and keep it right here, no matter what happens. If there seems to be a chance of your being caught, leave the car, but keep the spark plug in your pocket. Then they'll find it impossible to do much with it. It's too heavy to do much pushing, and I don't believe you're likely to be seen, anyhow, under the hedge here. We may have to make a mighty quick run for it if we get back here at all."

"Suppose you don't get away, Jack? Shall I wait here?"

"Wait until daylight, no longer. Not quite daylight, either. Let's see—figure to the sunrise, and wait till half an hour before that. And if you do have to go back alone, don't take any chances at all on being caught. Make even a wider circle than we did coming here, and don't go near Mardean. The car is a good deal more important than any of us. And don't forget, if you do have to leave the car and take to the woods, to take the spark plug with you. Do that, even if you just get out to get a drink at a well, or anything like that. Remember that we're right in the heart of the enemy's country, and you can't tell what minute you're likely to be attacked."

"All right, Jack. I don't believe they'll see me here, either. But I'll do the best I can if they do, and I'll be here, unless they pick me up and carry me away."

"That's the right spirit, Tom! I think you've got the hardest part of all. Pete and I've got something to do, and something pretty exciting, too. But you've just got to wait here in the dark for something to happen."

"Don't let it get on your nerves, Tom," said Pete. "It's hard work, but keep your nerve, and you'll be all right. Coming, Jack? So long, Tom!"

"So long, Pete and Jack! Good luck! I hope you'll get away from them all right—and get what you're after, too."

It was almost pitch dark by this time. The moon would not rise until very late, and the night had the peculiar blackness that sometimes comes before the moon appears. The country was thickly wooded here, which worked to the advantage of Jack and his companion. Most of the country in which Jack had been operating so far had been fairly open, which would have increased the difficulty of their task very much if the scene of operations had not been shifted eastward by the action near Newville that morning.

"How far are we from their headquarters now, Jack?" asked Pete.

"About a mile and a half, I think, Pete. I can't be sure, of course, but I think that's a pretty good guess. I could have run the car a little nearer and probably still been safe, but I didn't want to take chances. If we lose the car we can't get it back. If we're captured, why, they can get someone else to run the car, but we wouldn't be any good if we lost the machine."

"We'll want to be pretty careful, though, as we go along, Jack."

"Sure we will! But it won't be any harder than scouting the way we've learned to do, Pete. These people aren't looking for us, and we've done a lot of scouting when other fellows who were on the lookout for us knew just about where we were."

The lay of the land favored the two Scouts decidedly as they made their way onward. They were able to progress through the woods, but they did not have to go so deep into them that they could not observe, as they moved along, the situation in the open country that marched with the woods. In these fields they saw the twinkling of numerous fires, and they judged that the enemy was thick alongside, so to speak.

"They ought to watch these woods better than they do," whispered Jack. "Gee, I can see how their whole camp is laid out! That's one thing they're weak in—and it shows how important it is. They have fine strategy, but they're weak on details, like guarding their camp. If they don't watch these woods better when we start to make our get-away, we'll have it pretty easy."

"That looks like headquarters, Jack. See, over there?"

"You're right, Pete. And I'll bet they're planning to move before daylight, too. That's why 'Lights out!' was sounded so early. That was the call we heard about three quarters of an hour ago."

A light still showed in one of two big, adjoining tents, however, and the sound of voices came distinctly from it.

Jack waited until they were abreast of the tent.

"This will be a good place, Pete," he said. "There'll be a guard there. We want to pretend to make a run for it. Come on, now—make a little noise!"

Pete obeyed. The next moment the sharp challenge of a sentry rang out, and a shot followed. Jack and Pete ran, as if frightened and confused, right out into the midst of the sleeping men, and a moment later they were the prisoners of a group of laughing militiamen.

CHAPTER XII

A RACE FOR FREEDOM

"They've got us, Pete," said Jack, dejectedly.

"Here, who are you, and where did you come from?" said a sleepy officer, running up.

"We've caught a couple of spies, sir," said one of their captors.

"We are not spies!" cried Pete, indignantly. "Can't you see that we're in uniform?"

"Hello, that's an aggressive young fighter, all right!" said the officer, smiling at Pete's red-headed wrath. "No wonder—look at his hair! Boy Scouts, eh? Do you belong to Durland's Troop?"

"Yes, sir," said Jack.

"How did you get here?"

"I d—don't know, sir. We hadn't any idea we were right among you till we heard the sentry challenge us."

"Well, we won't eat you, my boy. No need to be frightened. Here, Corporal, put them in the guard tent. We haven't many prisoners—I guess we can take them along in the morning and let them see us lick the Reds at Tryon Creek."

Jack almost betrayed himself by the involuntary gasp he gave as the lieutenant revealed the secret he had taken so much trouble to surprise. Here was luck with a vengeance! The very information they wanted was being handed to them on a silver platter. But he managed to restrain his emotions, so that no one should suspect the elation he felt at the discovery.

Tryon Creek! That meant it was doubly important for the news to be carried back to General Harkness, for it showed that General Bliss had seized upon the weak spot in the Red line of defense, the necessity for weakening one spot to strengthen another, and, moreover, that the Blue army was far from being out of it as a result of the success of General Bean in the minor engagement of Tuesday morning.

Jack nudged Pete as they were being led away to the guard tent. And Pete nudged back, to show that he understood. That pleased Jack, for he knew now that the all-important information had a double chance of being carried to General Harkness. If he were baffled in his attempt to escape and Pete did manage to get away, the news would go with him.

"You two boys can give your parole in the morning," said the young officer. "The guard tent's the only place where there's room for you to-night, and anyhow you'll be just as comfortable there as if you'd given your parole."

Then he went off, leaving them to the care of the corporal of the guard, who seemed immensely amused. That relieved Jack, too. He had feared that they would be offered their parole, and that to refuse to give it would mean an added watchfulness on the part of their captors and jailers, as the Blue soldiers had become. Now he was relieved from that danger. It was lucky, he thought, that the officer was loose and careless in his methods.

In the guard tent they found themselves alone.

"Guess you can sleep all right in here," said the corporal. "It's a pretty comfortable prison, and there's lots of room. If you get lonely, call the sentry. He'll talk to you."

"Thanks," said Jack. "I'm sure you're very kind."

But he was really angry at the condescending way in which the Blue corporal spoke. As soon as he was alone with Pete he expressed his disgust, too.

"Gee, Pete," said he, "I thought this was going to be hard. It's like taking candy from a kid. They'll catch us if we go up to them and ask them please to do it, just the way we did before. And that corporal was acting as if we were little boys! I hope he finds out some time that we're the ones that spoiled their Tryon Creek plan for them."

"Hold on," said Pete, laughing. "We haven't done it yet, Jack. Gee, usually you're the one that keeps me from going off at halfcock. We're not out of the woods yet, old boy."

"That's right, too, Pete, but he did get my goat. He's so cocky! Some of our fellows are a little like that, too, I guess, but I haven't happened to run into any of them yet."

"I was just as mad as you were, Jack, but we have got a lot to do yet before we get back to Tom. How are we going to get out of here?"

"Cut our way out," he said, shortly. He looked back toward the flap of the tent in disgust. "They didn't even take our knives away from us. I wonder if they thought we were going to stay here like little lambs. And they didn't even ask us for our parole! I'll bet someone will get court-martialed for this— and they ought to, too."

Still looking his disgust, he began to cut through the stout canvas of the tent. As he had suspected, there was no sentry at all in the rear of the tent, and it was a matter of five minutes to cut a hole big enough to let them get out.

"Here we go, Pete!" he whispered. "We can get away now any time we want to. Might as well do it now, too. No use waiting any longer than we have to."

They slipped out quietly, within ten minutes of the time when they were put in the guard tent. Quietly still, and using every bit of Scout craft that they knew, they made their way to the shelter of the woods, wondering every minute why some alarm was not raised. But a dead silence still prevailed behind them when they crept into the sheltering shadow of the trees, and, once there, they straightened up and began to more fast.

First they went some distance into the woods, so as to lessen the danger of discovery should their absence from the tent be discovered, and then they struck out boldly in the direction which they had traveled only a short time before, making their way back toward the place where they had left Tom and the grey scout car.

"Gee," said Pete, drawing a long breath, "that certainly was easy! You were right, Jack. I thought they must be setting some sort of a trap for us. It didn't really seem as if they could be going to leave things fixed so nicely for us. Why, they might better have turned us loose at once! Then someone with more sense might have picked us up and really held on to us before we could get out."

"They ought to be licked for being so careless," said Jack. "I'll put everything that happened in the camp into my report. I'll bet the next time they get prisoners, they'll look after them all right! It makes me sore, because they're supposed to be learning how to act in case of a real war just as much as we are, and it shows that there's an awful lot of things they don't know at all."

In the east now the first faint stirrings of the light of the coming moon that would soon make the country light began to show.

"I'm glad we got through so soon, anyhow," said Jack, then. "For Tom Binns' sake, mostly. It must have been scary work for him, just sitting there in the dark, waiting for us."

"He won't have to wait much longer, Jack. He's certainly a plucky one! I know that waiting that way scares him half to death, but you never hear a peep out of him. He just does as he's told, and never whimpers at all."

"He's got what's really the highest courage of all, though he doesn't know it himself, Pete. He's got the pluck to do things when he's deadly afraid of doing them. There are a lot of people like that who are accused of being cowards, when they're really heroes for trying to do things they're afraid of. I've got much more respect for them than I have for people who aren't afraid of things. There's nothing brave about doing a thing you're not afraid of."

"There's the car now, Jack! We haven't wasted much time coming back, anyhow."

Jack put his hand to his lips and imitated the cry of a crow. That was the sign of the Crow Patrol, to which all three of the Scouts belonged.

"There comes his answer! That means the coast is clear. I was half afraid they might have caught him and the car. It wouldn't have done at all for us to escape as we have and then walk into a trap here—that would make us look pretty foolish, it seems to me."

"You're right it would, Jack. Hello, Tom! Anything doing here while we were gone?"

"Not a thing! How on earth did you get back so soon? Did you get what you were looking for?"

"I guess we did! Get the spark plug in, Tom, and we'll be off."

A few moments saw them on the road again, and moving fast. In the distance now, as they sped along, Jack's practiced ear caught a strange sound, and he slowed down so that he might listen the better.

"Say," he cried, in sudden excitement, "that's another car! And what's an automobile doing here at this time of night?"

The same thought came to the three of them at once.

"I wonder if it's one of their scout cars," cried Tom Binns, voicing the thought. "I've been thinking it was funny we hadn't run into them at all, Jack."

"Well, we'll have to look out if it is," said Jack.

The sound grew louder, and it was soon apparent that the other car was coming toward them. Jack slowed down, and kept to a slow pace, keeping his car as much as possible in the shadow of the trees that hung over one side of the road. The other car came on fast, and, as it swept around a bend of the road that had hidden it from them, they were almost blinded by the great ray from the searchlight it carried. Jack himself had been running without lights of any sort, for greater safety from detection.

As soon as the driver of the other car saw the machine in which the three Scouts were riding, he slowed down. It came alongside in a few moments and a man leaned out and hailed Jack.

"What are you doing here?" he cried, and then, before Jack could answer the question: "Come on, men, it's one of their cars! We've got to capture them!"

As he spoke he slewed his car around, so that it half filled the road, and two men leaped to the ground and made for Jack's car.

But Jack had a different plan. He had no mind to surrender tamely now when victory was within his grasp. In a moment the big grey car shot down the road, and the next moment it was roaring at full speed ahead. Behind it, after a stunned moment of surprise and silent inaction, thundered the other car, a scout car of the Blue army.

"Gee, this is going to be a real road race!" yelled Jack. "That car is this one's twin. They can go just as fast as we can. And they're stronger than we are, if they ever catch us—three men to three boys. But they'll have to go some to catch us!"

For the first time since his dash across the State line when the war began, Jack let the grey car do its best for him now. It leaped forward along the road as if it were alive. But behind, going just as fast, keeping the gap between the cars the same, pounded the hostile machine.

Over roads as empty as if they had been cleared by the police for a race for the Vanderbilt cup, the two cars sped, kicking up a tremendous dust, their exhausts roaring and spitting blue flame, and the noise of their passage making a din that Jack thought could be heard for miles. Only the big metal hood saved them from being cut to ribbons by the wind and the flying dirt and stones that their mad rush threw back from the road before them. But Jack had one big advantage, as he guessed. He knew the country better, and he was making baffling turns every few minutes. One thing he dared not do. He stuck to the road, afraid, at the frightful speed, to risk a side trip into the fields, and equally afraid to slow down, since that would mean that the other car, never very far behind, would be able to catch up to them.

So fast they went that, by making many corner turns, Jack was able to turn completely around without attracting the attention of the pursuing car. He was heading straight for Bremerton, finally, and his heart leaped at the thought that this new and unforeseen danger was going to be thrown off. Just to lose the car behind would not be enough, he knew. He was playing for high stakes now, and at last he slowed down—not much, but enough to let the other car make a perceptible gain. He felt safe now. He knew that the other car was no faster than his own, though it was just as fast, and if he had even a hundred yards of lead, he was sure he could hold it.

Other campfires were twinkling near by now. The sentries that guarded them, he knew, would not fail to hear and guess at the reason for the roaring race of the war automobiles.

And at last, making the sharpest sort of a turn, he baffled the pursuers. Before they realized what they were doing, they were in the midst of Colonel Abbey's regiment, and a minute later they were forced to stop by a volley of shots, and instead of capturing the Red scout car, as they had hoped, were themselves prisoners.

"I guess that's going some!" cried Pete, as they turned back toward the captured car. "We got the news we were after, and we led one of their scout cars into a trap, too. That's what I call a pretty good night's work. Fine business, Jack! And that was certainly some ride, too! If you hadn't been able to drive as well as you do, we'd never have got away from them."

"We had a lot of luck," said Jack. "But it certainly was a great race! I'll be glad to get some sleep, now. That was pretty tiring work."

CHAPTER XIII

A REAL ENEMY

Jack had led the hostile scout car into the most hopeless sort of a trap. He had twisted and turned and doubled on his course so cleverly that his pursuers had completely lost their sense of direction. In a chase of that sort, with his quarry in front of him, the driver of a racing automobile, making from sixty to seventy miles an hour, has no chance to watch objects about him.

There Jack's almost uncanny sense of direction and locality had helped him mightily. The speed at which he had driven his car had not at all confused him. He had known exactly what he was doing, and just where he was going, at all times. A few miles had taken him into country over which he had already driven, and his memory for any place he had once seen was phenomenal. So he had been able, by constant turning and doubling, to fool the driver of the enemy's car completely, and lead him, all unknowing the fate in store for him, into the very midst of the Red troops.

Jack had taken his final turn from the road so sharply that it had been impossible for his pursuer to turn quickly enough to follow him. Any attempt to do so would have resulted in disaster, and, since this was only a mock war, the driver of the other scout car was not justified in taking the chance of killing himself and his companions in the effort to make the turn. He had gone straight on, therefore, and a few rods had carried him into the midst of Abbey's cavalry regiment. A minute was enough to surround his car, and a line of troops in front of him made him see the hopelessness of escape. Therefore he stopped and surrendered.

Jack and his two companions sprang at once from their own car and ran quickly, glad of the chance to loosen their tired and aching muscles, stiff, sore and cramped from the confinement in one position that the wild race had forced, toward the group that was gathered around the captured car. Colonel Abbey, himself, the type of a true cavalry leader, was questioning the prisoners.

"I'm Captain Beavers, of the regular army," said the man who had driven the car, "detached from my regiment to serve on the staff of General Bliss. We were returning from a scouting trip in our car when we ran into this machine, and we chased it. The driver certainly knew his roads better than I did. I haven't had any idea for the last forty minutes of where we were going—I could only see the car ahead, and do all I could to catch it."

"How are you, Danby?" said Colonel Abbey, trying to hide a smile. "You'll excuse me, Captain, but you remind me a little of the dog that chased the railroad train. You know the old story about the farmer who watched him do it, and, when he got tired, turned around and said: 'What in tarnation do you reckon he'd do with that engine if he caught it?'"

Beavers laughed a bit ruefully.

"Something in that, Colonel!" he admitted. "I suppose it was a good deal like chasing a bird to put salt on its tail. But it was sheer instinct with us— nothing more. We saw that car start up, and we chased it. A fine lot of trouble it's got us into, too! But I guess we'd do the same thing again, probably."

"Any of us would, Captain," said Abbey. "Don't feel bad about it. We'll have to impound your car, but if you'll give me your parole, I'll be glad to give you the run of the camp."

"Thank you," said Captain Beavers. "I say, I'd like to see the man who led me that chase. I had an idea that I knew something about driving a fast car, but he can show me lots of things I never knew at all."

Suddenly his eye fell upon Jack Danby, whose hands gave abundant evidence that he was the chauffeur. The captain's jaw dropped and he stared at the Scout in amazement.

"You don't mean to tell me that it was you who was driving that car?" he gasped, finally.

"Permit me," said Colonel Abbey, smiling. "Scout Jack Danby, of Durland's Troop, Captain, and the operator of our first scout automobile ever since these maneuvers began."

"Well, I'll be jiggered!" said Beavers, speaking slowly. "You're all right, my boy! You drove that car like a Lancia. If you entered one of the big road races I believe you'd win it—upon my word I do!"

"We had a big lead at the start," said Jack; then, flushing a little at this public praise, "You see, the two cars are supposed to be exactly alike, and if one is just as fast as the other, and two of them get into a race, it's only natural for the one that has the start to keep its lead. I don't think I deserve any special credit for that. All I had to do was to keep her at full speed and steer."

"Yes, but it took more than that to lead us into this little man trap you had ready for us. Don't forget that!"

"Danby," said Colonel Abbey then, significantly, "you'd better get over to your headquarters and report to Captain Durland, if you have any information as a result of your trip. He is probably anxious to learn what you have accomplished."

Jack saluted at once, and turned on his heel. The headquarters of the Scouts was a mile or so distant from Abbey's camp, so the three Scouts got in the car again.

"Gee," said Jack, as he tested his gasoline tank, "we couldn't have gone much farther, that's sure! The juice is pretty low here, and if we had had to go a mile or so farther I don't know what might have happened. I guess he could have put the salt he was talking about on our tails easily enough."

"Well, he didn't, anyhow," said Tom Binns. "It isn't what they might have done, but what they did, that counts, Jack. I think we came out of it jolly well. Gee, but I was scared when that headlight hit us first!"

Durland was up and waiting for them when they arrived.

"Tryon Creek, eh?" said he, when Jack had made his report. "I thought as much. They may have weaknesses of their own in the matter of keeping a close guard, but General Bliss doesn't overlook anything in the way of strategy. He is mighty wide-awake on any point of that sort. I think I'll let you drive me over to General Harkness's headquarters and go in with you while you make your report in person, Jack."

General Harkness had to be awakened, but he had left orders that he was to be called at once should the Boy Scouts bring any news, and they had no difficulty in reaching him.

"You don't think there can be any mistake about their intention to march by way of Tryon Creek, do you?" he asked, with a grave face, when Jack had finished making his report.

"No, general, I do not," said Jack, and he explained the manner in which he had obtained his information.

"That lieutenant, you see, thought we were pretty well scared, and it never entered his head that we might try to escape," he said. "I've got an idea myself that they haven't found out yet that we've gone, really. There was no hue and cry raised while we were slipping out of their lines and back to the automobile, and I'm sure that we would have heard if there had been any pursuit. It's my idea that they won't discover that we're missing until breakfast. Even then, they're not likely to suspect that we know as much as we do, and I don't believe it will occur to that lieutenant to tell anyone that we learned from him where their attack was to be made. He'll probably forget that he said what he did."

"I hope so," said General Harkness. "In any case we will act on the information. If they knew that you had escaped with that news, I think General Bliss would be quite likely to change his plan. But I imagine that you are right about the officer who put you in the guard tent. His every action shows that he is careless and unlikely to think of the really important nature of the disclosure he made so lightly. I think we may assume with a fair amount of safety that they will attack by way of Tryon Creek, and I shall lay my plans accordingly and mass my troops at that point."

Jack had referred only incidentally to the race with the other car, but now the bell of the field telephone in the General's tent rang sharply, and an orderly answered it.

"Colonel Abbey, General," he said. "He wishes to know if he may talk to you."

Jack and Durland waited during the conversation that followed. General Harkness began laughing in a moment, and, after a conversation of five or six minutes, he hung up the receiver, his eyes wet with the tears his laughter had produced and his sides shaking.

"You leave out the most interesting part of your adventures when you think you can, don't you?" said he. "Do you know that Captain Beavers is regarded as the most expert driver of automobiles in the regular army? He invented the type of scout car that is being tried out, and you have beaten him squarely at a game that he should be the absolute master of."

"I hadn't heard a word about this," said Durland, showing a good deal of interest.

"I suppose we never would have from Danby," said the general. "That's what Abbey said—that was why he called me up."

And he proceeded to recount, while Jack, embarrassed, stood first on one foot and then on the other, the events that led up to the capture of the enemy's car, as Abbey had learned them from Captain Beavers. Far from being sore at his capture, Beavers regarded the whole affair as a fine joke on himself, and was only eager to find listeners who would give him a chance to repeat the story.

"That was fine work, Jack," said the Scout-Master, his eyes showing how proud he was of the Scout who had done his duty so well. "You accomplished something to-night that General Harkness and I were agreed was next door to impossible."

"It certainly seemed so to me," said the general, nodding his head. "But we needed that information badly, and I was ready to consent to any plan, however desperate the chances of success seemed to be, if it gave us even an outside chance to learn what it was that the enemy intended to do. We couldn't defend Tryon Creek and the Mardean road together, though we could block either one or the other, if we only knew where to look for the attack. As it is, thanks to what you have brought back, I think that we need have no fear of the outcome of the battle."

General Harkness, once aroused, and understanding what he had to do, stayed up. It was no time for him to sleep, and, as was presently proved, the army had had all the rest that was its due that night. For even as Jack and Durland made their way back to their own headquarters, the bugles began to blow, and the sleeping ranks began to stir all over the great encampment.

The transition from sleep to wakefulness and activity was brief enough. The bugles, blowing in all directions, aroused the sleepers, and soon all was bustle and apparent confusion all over the camp. But it was only apparent. Soon ordered ranks appeared, and all around the odor of frying bacon, and the aroma of coffee told of breakfast being cooked under the stars and the late moon, for it was recognized that there might be hard marching and plenty of it before there would be a chance for another meal. Two brigades were to start at once on the march to Tryon Creek, and General Harkness had ordered that the men eat their breakfast and receive a field ration before the march began.

"I guess we can turn in," said Jack to Pete and Tom, with a sigh of utter weariness. "Seems funny to be going to bed when everyone else is getting up—but they got in ahead of us on their sleep, so I guess it's our turn all right."

"Me for the hay, too!" said Pete Stubbs, without much thought for elegance of expression, but in such a tone as to convince anyone who heard him that he really needed sleep. As for Tom Binns, he hadn't been more than half awake since he had tumbled out of the car after the race, and he was leaning against a post, nodding, when the others aroused him to go upstairs.

The bustle and din of the army getting underway didn't keep Jack and his companions from sleeping. They cared little for all the noise, and even the rumbling of the gun caissons as the artillery went by was not enough to disturb them at all.

When Jack awoke it was broad daylight. He sprang to the window and looked out, to see that the sun was high, and that it must be after noon. In the distance the sound of firing told him that the troops were finding plenty of action. But the village street of Bremerton was deserted. There was no sign, except a litter of papers and scraps, that an army had ever disturbed the peace of the little border line village.

"Here, Pete, wake up!" he cried. "The whole army's gone—and we're left behind! Let's get dressed and see if there are any orders down below for us."

Pete got up, shaking his tousled red head disgustedly. He struggled over to the window, and a moment later a sharp cry from him brought Jack to his side.

"Jack! Look! Over there—looking up this way, now. See, it's Broom!"

Jack looked. There could be no doubt about it. The man who was lounging across the street was Broom, the villain who had escaped after Jack had caused his arrest at Wellbourne, and who had more than once tried to harm Jack and his friends.

"You're right, Pete," said Jack, quietly. "It's Broom!"

CHAPTER XIV

A PARLEY WITH THE ENEMY

Even Tom Binns, sleepy as he was, and hard as it usually was to arouse him, was wide awake as soon as he heard what his companions had seen.

"Broom!" he cried. "What's he doing here?"

"I don't know," said Jack, as he dressed hurriedly. "But I guess we'll soon find out, unless he's changed his ways. Whenever he appears it's a first-rate sign that there's trouble in the air. He's as good as a storm warning. Whenever you see him, look out for squalls, and you're not likely to be disappointed."

"He won't try to make any mischief here, with a whole army ready to drop on him if he starts anything," said Pete. "I believe he's all sorts of a scoundrel, and he's got plenty of nerve—but not enough for that."

"That's what we thought at the seashore, too, Pete, didn't we?" said Jack. "But he made trouble, all right, and it was only by good luck, really, that we got on to what he had in his dirty mind and stopped him."

"Yes, that's so, too, Jack. Gee, I wish I was a little bigger—I'd jump him myself and do all I could to lick him within an inch of his life!"

"What do you think we'd better do, Jack?" asked Tom.

"We've got to find out first what orders there are from Captain Durland. Then we can tell better. If Broom leaves me alone, I won't do anything about him. We're on active duty now, and we're not supposed to let any of our private affairs interfere with our duty. We're just as much bound to obey orders as if the country were really at war."

"I'm not worrying about interfering with him, Jack," said Pete, with a grin. "I'm perfectly willing to let him alone—in this State. His pull is in good working order here, you know. It wouldn't do any good, even if we did have him arrested. I don't believe he'd ever be taken back to Wellbourne for trial, because he and his gang know that there's a good chance that he might be sent to prison if he were ever taken there. But suppose he interferes with us? That's just what he's here to do, I think, if the way he always has acted is any guide to what he's likely to do now."

"Well," said Jack, "all we can do is to mind our own business and pay no attention to him at all, Pete, unless he bothers us. If he lets us alone, why, we'll do the same by him."

Then they went downstairs, and Jack found a note left for him by Durland.

"I have left orders that you are not to be awakened, unless you wake up yourselves, before three o'clock," the Scout-Master had written; "you three have had plenty of work, and you are entitled to a good rest. The Troop will be on scout duty near Tryon Creek, but your orders are to use the car, and reconnoiter in the direction of Mardean. The fighting will swing the Blue center over in that direction, unless we are badly beaten, and your orders are to keep a close watch on the roads leading to Fessenden Junction. It is possible that General Bliss may make a raid in that direction, probably with his cavalry brigade. Timely warning of any such plan is important, as it is not desirable to detach any considerable number of troops to guard the Junction."

"What would they want to make a raid toward the Junction for?" asked Pete, after Jack had shown him the note.

"Why not, Pete?"

"A cavalry brigade couldn't hold it a day, Jack. We would drive them out in no time at all. Don't you think so?"

"Well, even so, a day would be enough to do an awful lot of damage. They could destroy the station,—theoretically, of course,—tear up miles of track, burn all the cars there, and destroy or capture and carry off with them a great many of our reserve stores. That was why our capture of Hardport was such a blow to them. We didn't hold it very long, of course, but it wasn't much use to them when they got it back."

"I see, Jack. Yes, they could do a lot of mischief."

"You see, Pete, as it is now, even if we're beaten, we can fall back on the Junction, hold it with a relatively small force, and retreat on the capital and the inner line of defenses. But if our supplies and the railroad cars, and everything of that sort that are massed there were rendered useless by being marked destroyed, we couldn't do anything but make our way back toward the capital as best we could, with a victorious enemy harrying us all the way, which is a bad situation in warfare."

"Shall we cook breakfast for ourselves, Jack?"

"No! On account of Broom. Captain Durland will understand. We'll get our breakfast here. I think that's better. If he's waiting for us, we'll give him a good long wait, anyhow."

"Fine, Jack! I think that's a good idea, too. Gee, but I hate that man!"

"I can't say I exactly love him, myself, Pete. I wish I was big enough to have it out with him with my fists. That's certainly one fight that I wouldn't have any regrets for after it was over."

They had an excellent breakfast, and then they went out in the street together. Broom was still waiting, and save for one or two of the idlers commonly to be seen in a little country town, he was about the only person in sight. He came over toward them at once.

"Don't shoot, Colonel," he said to Jack, smiling amiably. "I ain't looking for no more trouble. I've been up against you and your pals often enough now to know that it don't pay to tackle you. You're too much class for me, and I'll give you best."

"We don't want to have anything to do with you," said Jack. "We know the sort of a man you are, and you'll get your deserts some time. But right now, if you'll let us alone, we'll do the same for you. We've got other things to do beside talk to you. Good-day!"

Jack really was rather relieved at Broom's pacific advances. He had not known what to expect from his enemy's appearance, and he knew that if Broom had any considerable number of his allies on hand, he and his companions would not be able to make a very effective resistance, try as they would. After all, they were only boys, though in some respects they had proved that they could do as well as men, and Broom and his fellows were grown men, without scruples, who had no idea, apparently, of what fair fighting meant. But though he was secretly pleased, he did not intend to let Broom see it, and moreover he felt that he must be constantly on the lookout for treachery.

"No use bearing malice and hard feelings," said Broom. "We never meant to hurt you, my boy. You'd have been safe enough with us, and, as you wouldn't come willing, we tried to get you to come the other way. We didn't do it, so you've got no call to be sore."

"I've had plenty of samples of your good intentions," said Jack, his lip curling in a sneer. "I'm not afraid of you, but you can't fool me with your soft, friendly talk, either. I know you, and all about you, and I'll thank you to keep away from us. We aren't going to stay here, anyhow, and we haven't got time to talk to you, even if we wanted to."

"Yes, you have!" said Broom, suddenly, coming close to Jack and dropping his voice. "Suppose I told you that I knew all about you, and could tell you who you were and everything else you want to know? You'd have had a better time at Woodleigh if you'd had a name of your own, like all the other fellows, wouldn't you? You know you would! Well, that's what I can do for you, if I want to. Now will you talk to me?"

"If you know all that about me, why don't you tell me?" asked Jack.

Despite himself, he was curious, and he was forced to admit that Broom interested him. The secret of his birth, which seemed resolved to elude him, was one that he would never tire of pursuing, and he was ready to make use of Broom, villain though he knew him to be, or anyone else who could shed some light on the mysterious beginnings of his life.

"I can't tell you now and here," said Broom. "But I tell you what I'll do. Meet me here to-night at eleven o'clock, if you're off duty, and I'll tell you the whole story. It's worth your while to hear it, too, I'll promise you."

"I'm likely to do that," said Jack, with a laugh. "Do you know that sounds like 'Will you walk into my parlor? said the spider to the fly.' You must certainly think I'm an easy mark if you think I'll go into a trap you set as openly as that! Not if I know myself!"

"You think you're mighty smart, don't you?" asked Broom, his face working with disappointment and anger. "I'm not setting any trap for you. If I'd wanted to do that, I couldn't have had a better chance than there was here this morning, when your Scouts and all the rest of your people went off and left you behind. If you're scared to come alone, bring anyone you like— Durland, Crawford, or anyone. Bring them all—the whole Troop! I don't care! But come yourself, or you'll always be sorry!"

Jack was impressed, despite himself, by the man's earnestness. He knew that Broom had been crooked in many ways, and he knew, also, that Captain Haskin, the railroad detective, had given him the reputation of being a clever criminal, whose scruples were as rare as his mistakes. But there was some truth in what the fellow said. Had he meant to make any attempt on Jack's liberty, he had already let the best chance he was likely to have for a long time, slip by.

"I'll think it over, and talk to Captain Durland about it," he said. "I won't promise to be here, but I may decide to come, after all."

"That's better," said Broom. "You think it over, and you'll see I'm right. If I wanted to hurt you, I'd have done it before this."

"One thing more, Broom. If I do come, I shall certainly not be alone. And if you try any tricks, it won't be healthy for you. I know you're not afraid of the law in this State, but I've got friends that won't be as easy on you as the police. And I'll have them along with me, too, if I come, to see that you don't forget yourself, and go back to some of your old tricks. If you're ready to take the chance, knowing that, I may come."

"You surely won't think of meeting him, will you, Jack?" asked Pete, in deep anxiety, after this conversation was ended and Broom had taken himself off. "I didn't offer to butt in, because I thought you could handle him better by yourself. But you won't let him take you in by just pretending that he's got something to tell you?"

"I shan't meet him alone, anyhow, Pete. But I don't know whether he's just pretending or not, you see. The trouble is this mystery about me is so hard to untangle that I hate to let even the slightest chance of doing so pass."

"I know, Jack, but please don't take any chances. You know what he's tried to do to you before, and I'm certain this is only some new trick. He's probably tickled to death to think that you didn't turn him down absolutely."

"I'll promise you one thing, anyhow, Pete. I won't make a move toward meeting him, nor have anything to do with him, without telling Dick Crawford and Mr. Durland about it first. And I won't do anything that they don't thoroughly approve of. Will that satisfy you?"

"Sure it will, Jack! Thanks! I hate to seem like a coward, but I'm a lot more afraid for you when you're in some danger than I would be if it were myself. That's why I'm so leery of this fellow Broom. I'm sure he means some sort of mischief, and I surely do hope that Mr. Durland and Dick Crawford will make you feel the same way about it that Tom Binns and I do."

"What, are you in on this, too?" asked Jack, with a smile, turning to little Tom Binns.

"I certainly am, Jack!" answered Tom. "I think Pete's quite right."

Then they got the car, and took the road for Mardean, prepared to turn back when they reached the right cross roads, and scout along toward Fessenden Junction.

Before them, on the other branch of the Mardean road, toward Tryon Creek, there had been heavy firing. That had gradually died away, however, and presently, as they sped on, they met a single soldier on horseback. It proved to be their friend, Jim Burroughs.

"Hello, Lieutenant!" called Jack, cheerily, as he stopped his car and saluted. "How is the battle going?"

"Fine and dandy," returned Jim Burroughs, reigning up his horse. "We got to Tryon Creek, and we licked them there. They didn't come along for more than two hours after we were in position. The umpires stopped the fighting after a while, and gave us the decision. I don't see how they're going to get through to Fessenden Junction, and, if we hold them on this line, they'll never get near enough to the capital even to threaten it, that's one sure thing!"

"I'm certainly glad we got the true news," said Jack, after Jim Burroughs had ridden on. "It would have been fierce if that fresh lieutenant had been wrong himself, and we had given our own army false information that would have enabled them to beat us. But it's all right, as it turns out, and I guess that they haven't got any chance at all of beating us now."

"I'm glad of that, too," said Pete. "We certainly took enough trouble to get the right dope, didn't we?"

CHAPTER XV

A DECISIVE MOVEMENT

Pete Stubbs was secretly glad that the scouting trip toward Fessenden Junction had been ordered. He was terribly afraid of the consequences to Jack should he accept Broom's defiance and meet him that night, and he did not know whether Durland and Dick Crawford would share his views. So he hoped that the work in the scout car would distract Jack's mind and lead him to forget his promise to Broom to see what the Scout-Master and his assistant thought of the plan.

As the car made its swift way along the roads towards Fessenden Junction, the sound of firing constantly came to them.

"I thought Jim Burroughs said the fighting had been stopped," said Tom Binns.

"The main bodies were stopped, but that doesn't mean the whole fight is over," explained Jack. "Bean's brigade, you see, probably hasn't been in action at all yet. His troops were not among those sent to Tryon Creek, and he has to cover the roads leading in this direction. It's just because General Harkness is afraid that some of the Blue troops may have been detached to make a raid by a roundabout route that we are coming over here."

"Suppose we ran into them, Jack? Would we be able to get word back in time to be of any use?"

"Why not? This is our own country. We have the telegraph and the telephone wires, and the railroad is within a mile of General Harkness's quarters at Tryon Creek. All he needs to do is to pack troops aboard the trains he undoubtedly has waiting there and send them on to Fessenden Junction. We have the same advantage here that the enemy had when they held Hardport. Then we had to move our troops entirely on foot while they could use the railroad, and move ten miles to our one. Now that position is reversed—as long as we hold the key of the railroad situation, Fessenden Junction."

The road to Fessenden Junction was perfectly clear. They rolled into the busy railroad centre without having seen a sign of troops of either army. A single company was stationed at the depot in Fessenden Junction, impatient at the duty that held it there while the other companies of the same regiment were at the front, getting a chance to take part in all the thrilling moves of the war game.

Jack told the officers all he knew as they crowded around his car while he stopped to replenish his stock of gasoline. There was little in his narrative that had not come to them already over the wires, but they were interested in him and in the scouting car.

"We've heard all about you," said a lieutenant. "You've certainly done yourself proud in this war! They tell me that the car will surely be adopted as a result of your success with it. Do you know if that's so?"

"I hadn't heard, Lieutenant," said Jack, his face lighting up. "But I certainly hope it's true. It's a dandy car!"

"You didn't expect to see anything of the enemy the way we came, did you, Jack?" asked Pete Stubbs, when they were in motion once more.

"No, I didn't, Pete. But it was a good chance to study a road we didn't know. We may have considerable work in this section before we get through, and I want to know the roads. That road, of course, is guarded this morning by General Bean's brigade. It would take more than a raiding cavalry brigade to break through his line and make for the Junction this way, and if General Bliss sent troops to Fessenden, they wouldn't stop to fight on the way. They would choose a road that was open, if they could, or very weakly defended, at least. Otherwise they'd be beaten before they got here. Even a couple of regiments would be able to hold up a brigade, no matter how well it was led, long enough for General Harkness to find out what was going on and occupy Fessenden Junction in force."

"Where are you going now, then?"

"East of Bremerton, on the way back. I know that isn't exactly orders, but it seems to me it's common sense. General Bliss had a long line this morning, and Mardean was practically its centre. Hardport had become his base again. He's held Hardport now for two days, practically, and he's had time to repair all the damage we did. Why shouldn't he have thrown his brigade, if he planned a raid on the Junction at all, thirty miles east from Hardport, to swing across the State line at about Freeport, cut the railroad east of Fessenden Junction, and so approach it from the east, when everyone expects an attack to be made from the west?"

"That would be pretty risky, wouldn't it, Jack?"

"Certainly it would—and yet, if he could fool everyone into thinking he was going to do just the opposite, it would be the safest thing he could do. You see, all the fighting to-day has been well west of Bremerton and Fessenden Junction. Our orders were to do our scouting on the western side of the Junction. I've obeyed those orders, and I haven't found out a thing. Now I think I've a right to use my own discretion, and see if there are signs of danger on this side."

"Gee, that certainly sounds reasonable, Jack! They've been doing the thing that wasn't expected ever since the business started. I guess they're just as likely as not to keep on doing it, too."

"We ought to know in a little while, anyhow, Pete. I'm going to circle around here, strike a road that runs parallel to the railroad as it runs east of the Junction, and see what's doing."

Jack hurried along then for a time, and none of those in the car had anything to say, since, when Jack was pushing her, the noise was too great to make conversation pleasant or easy in any sense of the words.

They were in the road now that ran along parallel with the railroad that, running east from Fessenden Junction and away from the State capital, which lay southwest of that important point, approached gradually a junction with the main line of the railroad from Hardport at Freeport.

Jack was keeping his eyes open. He hardly knew what he expected to see, but he had an idea that there would be something to repay their trip.

And, about fifteen miles from Fessenden Junction, the soundness of his judgment was proved once more.

"Look up there!" cried Pete, suddenly. The eyes of three Scouts were turned upward in a moment, and there, perhaps two miles away, and three hundred feet above them, they saw a biplane hovering.

"Gee!" cried Jack. "That's the first we've seen in the air—a Blue biplane! None of our machines would be in this direction."

Swiftly he looked along the fence until he saw an opening.

"Here, jump out and let those bars down!" he cried, stopping the car.

The others obeyed at once, and in a moment he ran the car gently into the field and stopped beside a hayrick.

"Sorry to disturb the farmer's hayrick," said he, then, jumping out in his turn, "but this is important!"

And a moment later the three Scouts, following his example, were as busy as bees, covering the grey automobile with new hay, that hid it effectually from any spying eyes that might be looking down on them from above.

"Now we'll make ourselves look small," said Jack.

He looked around the field.

"I shouldn't wonder if they picked this out for a landing spot, if they decide to land at all," said he. "We want to see them if they do anything like that, and hear them, too, if we can. We may want to find out something from them."

Swiftly, then, they burrowed into the hay. They could look out and see anything that went on about them, but unless an enemy came very close, they themselves were entirely safe from detection.

"Now we'll know what they're up to, I guess," said Jack, with a good deal of satisfaction. "It's a good thing I sort of half disobeyed orders and came this way, isn't it?"

"You didn't really disobey orders, did you, Jack?" asked Tom.

"No, I didn't, really, Tom. I did what I was ordered to do, but I did something more, too, as there was no special time limit set for the job they gave us. But a scout is supposed to use his own judgment a good deal, anyhow. Otherwise he wouldn't be any use as a scout, so far as I can see."

It was very quiet in the hay. But above them, and sounding all the more clearly and distinctly for the silence that was everywhere else, they could hear the great hum of the motor of the aeroplane. With no muffler, the engine of the flying-machine kicked up a lot of noise, and, as it gradually grew louder, Jack was able to tell, even without looking up, that it was coming down.

"By George," said he, "I think they are going to land! They're getting more cautious, you see. They scout ahead now, and they're using their war aeroplane the way we have been using this car of ours."

"What are our flying-machines doing, Jack? I haven't seen them on the job at all."

"General Harkness is using them in the actual battles. They go up to spot concealed bodies of the enemy, so that our gunners can get the range and drive the enemy, theoretically, out of any cover they have found. That's one of the ways in which flying machines are expected to be most useful in the next war. You see, as it is now, with smokeless powder and practically invisible uniforms, ten thousand men can do a lot of damage before anyone on the other side can locate them at all. But with a flying-machine, they won't be able to hide themselves. A man a thousand feet above them can see them, and direct the fire of artillery by signals so that the troops that were in entire security until he discovered them can be cut to pieces by heavy shell fire."

"That's what our men have been doing, eh?"

"Yes—and theirs, too, mostly. This is the first time I've seen one of their machines scouting. Look out now—keep quiet! They're landing, and they're not more than a hundred feet away!"

The scraping of the flying-machine, as it came to rest in the field, was plainly audible as the Scouts stopped talking and devoted themselves to listening intently. Also, by craning their necks a little, though they were in no danger of being seen themselves, they could make out what the two men in the aeroplane were doing.

"Pretty lucky, Bill!" said one of them. "This is a good landing-place, and we can get an idea of the situation and cut the telegraph wire to send back word."

"Right, Harry!" said the other. "I guess the coast is clear. The brigade isn't more than five miles back, and with three train loads, they'll be able to make that Fessenden Junction look like a desert before night—theoretically."

"It's all theory, Bill, but it's pretty good fun, at that. I tell you, we would be in a tight place if they'd guarded this approach at all. That brigade of ours would be cut off in a minute. But if we can mess up Fessenden Junction for them, they'll be so busy trying to cover their line of retreat that they won't have any time to bother about our fellows."

"What's the matter with that engine, anyhow?"

"Nothing much, I guess. But sometimes, if she starts missing, the way she did when we were up there, you can fix things and avoid a lot of trouble by a little timely tinkering. I was up once when my engine began missing that way, and I didn't pay any attention to it. Then, about twenty minutes later, she went dead on me while I was over the water, and I had to drop, whether I wanted to or not. The water was cold, too, I don't mind saying."

"You hear that?" said Jack, in a tense whisper. "Now, as soon as they go, we've got to destroy that railroad track, right across the road. We may have half an hour; we may have only a few minutes. And while two of us do that—you and Tom, Pete—the other will have to cut the telegraph wire and send word to Fessenden Junction. General Bean is in the best position to get over there. I don't think we can hold them up more than an hour or so, but that ought to be enough. At least, if there's nothing else to be done, the fellows at Fessenden Junction can tear up a lot of track."

For five breathless minutes they watched the two aviators tinkering with their engine. Then the big bird rose in the air again, and winged its way eastward. In a moment Jack was out of the hay and calling to his companions to follow him.

"Get your tools from the car, now," he said. "Mark a rail torn up for every ten minutes you spend there. I'll get busy with the telegraph wire."

It took Jack twenty minutes to finish his task, which was exceedingly quick work. But he had had practice in it, and he worked feverishly, since he did not know at what minute they would be surprised and forced to abandon the task by the on-coming enemy.

Ten minutes after he had completed his part of the task, when, theoretically, the others had been able to destroy three lengths of rail, and had left a pile of smouldering brushwood as proof that they had had time to build a fire of the ties, they heard the hum of approaching trains along the rails.

"All right!" cried Jack. "This is as far as they can go now until they make repairs. It's time for us to be off!"

And he led the way swiftly toward the car, still hidden in the field.

Swiftly he adjusted the spark plug, which he had carried with him, and, just as the first of the trains from the east appeared in sight, the car was ready to move. But Jack, instead of returning to the road, and retracing his course toward Fessenden Junction, headed north across the field, toward the State line.

"I'm going to take a short cut to General Bean's brigade and get him word of the chance he has to end things right now," he cried. "If he can capture this brigade of the enemy, the war will be as good as over. It's the best chance we've had yet."

Jack knew the country perfectly, and soon he was on a country road, which, while it would have been hard on the tires of an ordinary car, was easy for the big scouting machine. They made splendid time, and in an hour they were in touch with the outposts of General Bean's troops, waiting, since the attack of the enemy in front had ceased, for any news that might come.

"I've just heard that the enemy is threatening Fessenden Junction from the east," the general told Jack, when the Boy Scout made his report.

"Yes, General," said Jack, eagerly. "And the roads are open in this direction. They will not be able to get very far along the railroad. The troops in Fessenden Junction will undoubtedly cut the tracks, just as we did, somewhere near the village of Bridgeton, and that will be a splendid place to make a flank attack. They won't be expecting that at all, and I think you can finish them up."

General Bean reached at once for a field map.

"You've got it!" he cried. "That's just what I'll do!"

And in a moment he had given his orders accordingly. Ten minutes later the troops were on the march, and Jack was scouting ahead, to make sure that no shift of the enemy's plan had made it impossible for his idea to be carried out successfully.

Bean's troops marched quickly and well, and within two hours they were in touch with the enemy, near Bridgeton. Jack and his companions, in the rear, heard the sound of firing, which soon became general. And then, unhampered, Jack sped for the place where he had already cut the railroad, and, in two hours theoretically destroyed nearly half a mile of track.

"They're in a trap, now," he cried. "They'll never get by here!"

CHAPTER XVI

THE PERIL IN THE WOODS

It was nearly seven o'clock that evening, and quite dark, when Jack and the others rejoined the main body of the Troop of Scouts at Bremerton.

Durland was full of enthusiasm.

"The war is as good as over," he said, happily. "We've licked them utterly! It's just a question now of what they'll be able to save from the wreck. The brigade that made the raid toward Fessenden Junction was annihilated by Bean, cut off, and forced to surrender. General Bliss is in full retreat upon Hardport from Mardean, and the invasion has been repelled. Our cavalry is pursuing him, and I think we will be in Hardport again to-morrow. Whatever fighting remains to be done will be on their side of the line, and the capital is safe."

"Will there be any more fighting to-night, Captain?" asked Jack.

"Only by the cavalry. They are worrying Bliss as much as possible in his retreat, and we'll probably pick up a few guns. We outnumber them decidedly now, as we have taken nearly eleven thousand prisoners in the last two days, and there is no chance at all for them to take the offensive again. General Bliss will be lucky to escape the capture of his whole army. One of the umpires told me to-day that our success was due entirely to the speed and accuracy with which we got information of the movements of the enemy, which seemed to him to be remarkably well covered."

"That's what Jack Danby's done for us," said Dick Crawford. "He's certainly proved that the scout car has come to stay. And it was more or less by accident that he got the chance to handle it, too."

"That's true," said Durland, "but a great many men have opportunities just as good, and can't make use of them. It's not how a man gets a chance to do things that counts, it's the way he uses the chance when he gets it. And that's where Jack's skill and courage have helped him. You've covered the Troop with glory, Jack, and we're all proud of you."

"Is there anything more for us to do to-night, sir?"

"No, indeed! I think everyone feels that the Boy Scouts have done rather more than their share already in the fighting we've had, and have been very largely responsible for our victory. There may be more work to do to-morrow, but I doubt it. I think myself that the umpires will call the invasion off to-morrow, and devote the rest of the time to field training for both armies, working together.

"About all the lessons that the war can teach have been learned by both sides already, and the training is useful, even when the war game itself is over. That's only a guess, of course, but if we are in a position to-morrow that leaves General Bliss as small a chance for getting away as seems likely now, I think the umpires will feel that there is no use in going through the form of further fighting. We are masters of the situation now, and our superiority in numbers is so great that there will be very little that is instructive about a further campaign."

Then Jack asked Captain Durland and Dick Crawford if he could speak to them apart, and when the Scout-Master consented, he told them of his interview with Broom.

"That's a queer shift for him to make," said Durland, thoughtfully. "It's true, of course, that he was in a good position to make an attack on you this morning. But it's also possible that he was alone, and didn't have any help handy. I don't think he'd ever try any of his dirty work single-handed. He's a good deal of a coward, and he likes to have a lot of help when he tries anything, so that there is practically no chance for his opponent. His idea is to fight when he is in overwhelming force, and only then. What do you think of it, Dick?"

"I don't trust him, sir, and yet, if it is at all possible that he has given up his designs against Jack and is willing to tell him what we are so anxious to find out, it would be a great pity to let the chance slip."

"That's what I think, sir," said Jack. "Pete Stubbs and Tom Binns heard him, and they think I ought not to meet him. But I'm afraid he's right, and that if I didn't do it, I'd always regret it."

"It seems safe enough," said Durland. "He didn't insist on your meeting him alone. He probably knew that you wouldn't do that, anyhow, and took the only chance he had of persuading you, but I don't see what harm could come to you if you went to meet him with Dick Crawford and myself, and perhaps two or three others, to see that there was no foul play."

"It's risky to have any dealings with him at all, I think," said Dick Crawford, "but if it was ever safe, I should say that this was the time. He's an awfully smooth scoundrel, or he wouldn't have been able to fool the Burtons the way he did. Still, it's hard, as you say, sir, to see what harm could come to Jack to-night."

"I think it's worth risking, anyhow," said Durland. "You and I will go along, Dick. And I think I'll have a talk with Jim Burroughs, too. It might be that he would feel like coming along with us."

"Can I bring Pete Stubbs and Tom Binns with us, sir?" asked Jack. "I think they'd like to be along."

"By all means," said Durland.

Jack went off then to look for his two chums. But they were nowhere to be seen. He was surprised, for, since they were on active duty, they were supposed to be always in readiness at the headquarters of the Troop unless detached with special orders. Finally, after hunting for them for half an hour, he asked Bob Hart about them.

Bob, who, as Patrol Leader of the Crow Patrol, ranked during the maneuvers as a sergeant, seemed surprised.

"I gave them permission to be absent from headquarters until eleven o'clock," he said. "Didn't you know they were going to ask for it?"

"I did not," said Jack, decidedly surprised.

Pete and Tom had known of the chance that he might meet Broom, and he wondered how it was that they were willing to be absent at a time when he might need them. It was the first time either of them had ever failed him, and he was puzzled and bothered by their absence.

"That's certainly mighty queer!" he said to himself. "I wonder if they forgot about Broom, or if they thought I would?"

But there was no sense in trying to puzzle out the reason for their having gone. They were off—that was plain, and he would have to go without them.

While he waited for Durland and Dick Crawford to return, he began to speculate a good deal as to what the reason for Broom's new shift might be. He was sure, from the way Broom had acted, that the man was as much his enemy as ever. And yet he had seemed to feel that he and Jack together might be able to accomplish something that was beyond the power of either of them, alone, to get done.

"Perhaps he's had trouble of some sort with the people who want to keep me from finding out about myself," thought Jack. "In that case, he's simply turned traitor to them, and is trying to use me to get even with them. Well, I don't care! They must be a pretty bad lot, and if I can find out about myself I don't see why I should mind helping him to that extent. But I'd certainly like to know the answer!"

He waited some time longer before the Scout-Master and Dick Crawford returned.

"Jim Burroughs isn't there," said Dick, with a puzzled expression on his face. "His captain says that he and several of the men got leave before dinner, because they wanted to see if they couldn't pick up some birds a little way off, in a preserve that belongs to a man who is a friend of Jim's. But we went over in that direction, and there wasn't any sign of them."

"Well, it's no great matter, anyhow," said Durland, with a smile. "There are enough of us left to attend to the matter. We'd better be getting along, Jack. Where are Stubbs and Binns?"

"They got leave for a little while from Sergeant Hart, sir," said Jack. "That seems mighty funny to me, because they knew about Broom, and that I might want them along with me to-night."

"They've probably forgotten it, Jack," said Dick. "You've all had a pretty full day and things slip the mind sometimes in such circumstances. No use worrying about them. We'll go ahead, anyhow."

At the place where Broom had made his appointment a man was waiting for them.

"Mr. Broom said this place was too public," the man whispered. "If you'll come along with me, I'll show you where he is waiting for you now."

"We'll come," said Durland. "But look here, my man, no tricks!"

He drew his hand from his holster, and showed the guide, a sullen, scowling fellow, the big pistol that reposed there.

"If I see any sign of treachery, I'm going to use this and see who's to blame afterward," Durland went on, grimly. "You'd better play level with us, or you'll have a mighty good reason to regret it. That's a fair warning, now. See that you profit by it. The next will be from my pistol!"

"Aw, g'wan, what's eatin' youse?" asked the man. But, despite his bluster, he was obviously frightened.

"I ain't here to hoit youse," he said, sullenly, after a minute's silence. "Just youse come along wid me, and I'll take youse to Broom. That's all the job I got, see?"

He led them some distance into the woods. Once or twice they thought they heard sounds as if others were near them, but they made up their minds that this idea was due to their imaginations. And finally, when they were nearly two miles from the nearest troops, as far as they could tell, their guide stopped in a little clearing in the woods.

"Wait here," he said. "I'll go tell Broom you're ready."

He crashed off through the undergrowth, and, with what patience they could, they waited in the darkness.

They realized afterward that the waiting was a blind. No one had crept up on them, but they were suddenly seized, each one from behind, so that there was no chance at all for Durland and Crawford to use the pistols that they held in their hands. Their assailants, as they guessed later, had been waiting all the time for them, ready to spring, upon them as soon as they were thoroughly off their guard. And in a moment they saw Broom, an electric torch in his hand, which he directed at the faces of the three prisoners in turn.

"You walked into the trap all right, didn't you?" he said to Jack, with an ugly sneer on his face. "You was mighty smart this morning! Glad you brought your friends along. They've bothered us, too. And now we've caught you all together. That's much better, you see! You won't get in my way again, any one of you!"

Suddenly he gave a curse.

"Where's the others?" he snarled. "The red-headed one and the little shaver? I want them, too!"

"There weren't but the three of them," said the man who had served as their guide. "I don't know where the others are."

"Well, it can't be helped," said Broom, with an oath. "I'll get rid of these, anyhow."

"You'll spoil no more games of mine!" he told them. "Get the ropes, there, men!"

"What are you goin' to do?" asked one of Broom's men.

"String them up," replied Broom, with a brutal laugh. "Hanging leaves no evidence behind. No weapons—no wounds to show the sort of a blow that killed. There's good advice for you, my friend. If you want to get rid of an enemy, hang him!"

All three of the prisoners had been gagged. They had to stand silent, now, while the rope was placed about their necks. They were all forced to stand under the spreading branch of a big tree, and the ropes were thrown over it.

"We'll let them swing all together, now," said Broom. "When I give the word! Plenty of time, though! We'll let them have a minute or two to think it over."

"NOW!" cried a voice in the woods beyond the small circle of light from Broom's electric torch.

A second later the click of falling hammers fell on the air. And, even as Broom turned, a dozen men stepped into the light, with leveled rifles, covering every one of the gang that Broom had gathered to make his trap.

"Fire if they make a single movement!" ordered Jim Burroughs. "Good work, Pete! Release them now! You brought us here—it's only fair to let you turn them loose, you and Tom Binns."

"Go ahead and shoot!" yelled Broom, suddenly, and made a dash for the woods. A dozen rifles spoke out, but he crashed away in the darkness, and one or two of the others ran also.

"He got away!" said Durland. "Pretty bad shooting, Jim!"

"Well, you can't expect much from blank cartridges," said Jim Burroughs, with a grin. "We didn't have any loaded with ball, you know. It was just a bluff, but it worked pretty well!"

"But how did you get here at all?"

"Pete Stubbs and Tom Binns are responsible for that. They didn't like the idea of this expedition at all, and neither did I, when they told me about it. We stuck pretty close to you. But I wanted to make sure of Broom, or I'd have butted in before."

9 781836 572381